"What's going on?"

Tori asked from the doorway.

Adam turned and looked at her, his brown eyes sparking with sudden recognition. "You're an FBI agent?" he asked in a deadly, quiet voice.

Tori's mouth parted softly on a gasp. "Adam! What are you doing here?"

"That seems to be the question of the moment, doesn't it?"

Her throat closed with emotion. "Oh, God, I didn't want you to find out this way."

His dark eyes were unwavering, as cold as his tone. "What way did you have in mind? Perhaps morning-after pillow talk?"

"You know better than that," she said quietly. "I didn't want you to find out at all. That's why I left before anything could happen between us."

"Then you left a little late."

Dear Reader:

The spirit of the Silhouette Romance Homecoming Celebration lives on as each month we bring you six books by continuing stars!

And we have a galaxy of stars planned for 1988. In the coming months, we're publishing romances by many of your favorite authors such as Annette Broadrick, Sondra Stanford and Brittany Young. Beginning in January, Debbie Macomber has written a trilogy designed to cure any midwinter blues. And that's not all—during the summer, Diana Palmer presents her most engaging heros and heroines in a trilogy that will be sure to capture your heart.

Your response to these authors and other authors of Silhouette Romances has served as a touchstone for us, and we're pleased to bring you more books with Silhouette's distinctive medley of charm, wit and—above all—romance.

I hope you enjoy this book and the many stories to come. Come home to romance—for always!

Sincerely,

Tara Hughes
Senior Editor
Silhouette Books

BRITTANY YOUNG

A Matter of Honor

Silhouette *Romance*

Published by Silhouette Books New York

America's Publisher of Contemporary Romance

SILHOUETTE BOOKS
300 E. 42nd St., New York, N.Y. 10017

ISBN: 0-373-08550-8

First Silhouette Books printing January 1988

America's Publisher of Contemporary Romance

Printed in the U.S.A.

Books by Brittany Young

Silhouette Romance

Arranged Marriage #165
A Separate Happiness #297
No Special Consideration #308
The Karas Cup #336
An Honorable Man #357
A Deeper Meaning #375
No Ordinary Man #388
To Catch a Thief #424
Gallagher's Lady #454
All or Nothing #484
Far From Over #537
A Matter of Honor #550

BRITTANY YOUNG

lives and writes in Racine, Wisconsin. She has traveled to most of the countries that serve as the settings for her Romances and finds the research into the language, customs, history and literature of these countries among the most demanding and rewarding aspects of her writing.

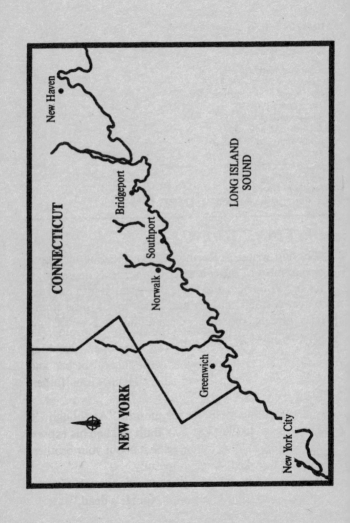

Chapter One

Adam Danaro stood looking through the hospital window at the unfinished skyscraper across the street that he himself had designed, but he wasn't really seeing it. He dragged his fingers through his dark hair tiredly and turned back to the shadowed room. The eyes of the old man in the bed were open, watching him. Adam sat in the chair by the side of the bed and took the old man's hand in his. "Hello, Grandfather. How are you feeling?"

A weak smile touched his mouth. "As though I'd been kicked in the chest by a mule." Then his expression changed. "I didn't imagine it about your brother, did I?" he asked almost hopefully.

A muscle in Adam's jaw moved, though his face showed no visible emotion. "No. He's dead."

"Do you know who did it?"

"The word on the street is that it was Angelo Fortuna."

Salvatore sighed. His eyes drooped shut for a moment, but then he opened them again and focused intently on Adam. "There must be no reprisal."

Adam said nothing.

"There are things that must be taken care of before I die. The other families are already hovering like vultures over the spoils."

"I'll handle everything, Grandfather."

"I know." He gazed at this grandson he'd raised like one of his own children. This grandson who was the most like him. Strong-willed and independent with a cool head and sharp mind that could cut straight to the heart of problems. "It's taking so much time, Adam. So much time. More than I ever thought it would when I asked for your help."

"Don't worry about it. We'll get there."

"Imagine, Salvatore Danaro, a legitimate businessman."

"Stranger things have happened."

"But I haven't heard of them." Salvatore grew thoughtful. "But your own work—"

"Don't worry about my work," Adam interrupted. "Don't worry about anything. I'll stay with you until we finish what we started."

The old man let out a long breath as though he could at last relax. His eyes closed and a moment later his breathing was deep and even.

Adam leaned back in the chair and studied the pale, drawn face against the hospital-white pillow. Anyone looking at him now would never believe that this frail man was the head of one of the largest crime syndicate families on the East Coast.

Adam couldn't remember a time when he hadn't known exactly who and what his grandfather was, but he'd had a hard time fitting the newspaper reports about Salvatore Danaro to the gentle man who'd raised him and his brothers and sister. He'd never turned his back on his grandfather; just his way of life.

And yet here he was, right in the middle of things. It was as though he'd never left. Adam rose from the chair and walked back to the window.

Salvatore opened his eyes. "Adam," he said in a whisper.

The younger man walked back to the bed.

"I'm glad you're here."

Adam's expression softened as he took his grandfather's hand in his. "Get some sleep."

"You should, too."

"I will when I get tired."

But Salvatore couldn't close his eyes. "I'm sorry about this. I know you don't want any part—"

Adam stopped Salvatore from finishing the sentence. "What I want," he said slowly, "is for you to get better, and that's not going to happen if you insist on talking rather than resting."

"Sometimes I think it would be best if I just let nature take her course."

"What are you talking about?"

"The FBI. They're coming at me from all angles." He smiled wearily. "The joke would be on them if I died before they could do anything with all of their hard work."

"I'll take care of the FBI."

"Can't be done."

"It will be done. They won't be bothering you anymore. Rest now."

Salvatore nodded as his fingers tightened on his grandson's hand. "You're right, you're right. I'll sleep now."

Adam said nothing, but squeezed his grandfather's hand in return, filling the old man with a sense of wellbeing. He was asleep within minutes.

When the telephone next to her bed rang, Victoria Burton tried to ignore it, but it was insistent. Still lying on her stomach with her eyes closed, she groped in the dark and finally found the receiver. Turning her head so that one ear was against the pillow, she held the receiver to her other ear and sighed before speaking. "Hello."

"Tori, this is Charlie."

"Charlie who?"

"Charlie, your boss," he said dryly.

Tori opened one eye and looked at the illuminated digital clock on her bedside table, then closed it again as she rolled onto her back with a rustle of sheets. "Do you have any idea what time it is?" she asked, her voice husky.

"Two-thirty," he answered promptly, "and the temperature is forty-five degrees with warmer temperatures expected later in the day."

She smiled at his sarcastic tone. "Thank you for that report. May I go back to sleep now?"

"I want you to get dressed and come to the office."

The deadly seriousness of his voice woke her the way nothing else could have. Tori raised up on an elbow and pushed her wavy mane of dark hair away from her face. "What's going on?"

"I'll tell you when you get here. How long will it take you?"

She looked at the clock again. "Thirty minutes."

"Make it twenty-five."

Tori hung up without saying goodbye, then stretched to turn on the lamp. Sitting on the edge of her bed, she narrowed her blue eyes and blinked a few times while her eyes adjusted to the light. Making her way to the bathroom, she soaked a washcloth in cold water and held it against her face. There was no time for makeup, but she managed to get a brush through her hair before tossing on a pair of jeans and an oversized white sweater.

Walking quickly through her apartment, she grabbed her car keys from the hall table and headed across Washington to the building that housed the Federal Bureau of Investigation.

When she got there, she went straight to Charlie's office. He was sitting behind his desk, leaning comfortably back in his chair. His hands were clasped behind his balding head, and he was talking to a tall, dark-haired man who stood in the shadows looking out the window.

"Charlie?" she said from the doorway. "What's going on?"

The stranger turned and looked at her, his brown eyes sparking with sudden recognition. "You're an FBI agent?" he asked in a quiet voice.

Tori's mouth parted softly on a gasp. "Adam! What are you doing here?"

"That seems to be the question of the moment, doesn't it?"

Her throat closed with emotion. "Oh, God, I didn't want you to find out this way."

His dark eyes were unwavering, as cold as his tone. "What way did you have in mind? Perhaps morning-after pillow talk?"

"You know better than that," she said quietly. "I didn't want you to find out at all. That's why I left before anything could happen between us."

"Then you left a little late."

"You two know each other?" Charlie asked, his interested eyes darting from one to the other.

Tori turned on him. "You know perfectly well that we know each other. Why did you bring him here?"

"All in good time, all in good time." The phone rang and Charlie answered it.

Tori could feel Adam's eyes on her. She forced herself to turn and meet his look with a direct one of her own. "I'm sorry."

"Well, that just makes everything all right, doesn't it?"

Charlie put his call on hold and hung up. "Excuse me, you two," he said as he left his office. "I'll be back in a minute."

Adam's eyes never left her. "So what's your real name? I know it's not Fields. I had some of the best detectives in the country looking for Victoria Fields and they all came up empty."

"It's Burton. Victoria Burton. You had detectives looking for me?"

"From the day you left me nearly a year ago until this moment. But of course they couldn't find you. They were looking for a woman who didn't exist." The muscle in his jaw moved again. "*I* was looking for a woman who didn't exist."

Tori said nothing. There wasn't any way she could defend herself.

His eyes raked over her slender figure. "So, what was I? A case you happened to be working on?"

"Something like that."

"Something exactly like that."

Silence fell between them until Adam broke it.

"Our meeting on the plane was planned by you?"

"Yes."

"Well—" he inclined his head "—my congratulations. You're very good at your job."

Tori's heart ached. "Adam, you have to understand that I—"

Charlie walked back in at that moment. "Take a seat, Tori."

She automatically sat down, her eyes still on Adam. The last time she'd seen him had been a little over a year earlier. He hadn't changed much; he was tall and athletic-looking with his dark hair neatly trimmed in the front, but longer in back so that it curled slightly over his shirt collar. He was very handsome, but it was an interesting kind of handsome.

"Do you want some coffee?" Charlie asked her.

Tori took her eyes off of Adam and pulled her thoughts back to the moment. "I'd appreciate it."

He got it himself from a pot on a table, handed her the mug then walked back behind his desk and sat down.

Tori took a sip and delicately wrinkled her nose. "How old is this stuff?"

"It was fresh this morning."

"You mean it was fresh yesterday morning."

"Whatever. Drink it. It's good for you. It'll put hair on your chest," he said absently, apparently forgetting that he wasn't talking to one of his sons.

"Something to look forward to." She took a sip, still intensely aware of the man so near but keeping her attention focused on her boss. "Now, will you please tell me what's going on here?"

"I'd be happy to. In a minute. Do you know anything about the Danaro family?"

Tori looked at him curiously. He knew better than anyone else that she'd been working on gathering evidence against Salvatore Danaro for more than two years. "Yes," she finally answered.

"I want you to share your most recent information with us."

Her eyes went to Adam, still standing silently by the window. "But, Charlie . . ."

He lifted his hand. "Just the highlights. Come on."

Tori wondered what he was up to. "All right. As Salvatore has gotten older, the members of his extended family have gotten restless. They don't know who's going to inherit the power. His only son—" she looked at Adam "—your father, is dead. And until two years ago, you didn't seem interested. But current information has it that you're now very comfortably ensconced in your grandfather's old office conducting business as usual with the Atlantic City casinos and his Las Vegas interests. It's believed that you're now the heir to the throne, Adam. But not everyone is happy about that."

The man's brown eyes gazed into her blue ones. "For instance?" he asked.

"Angelo Fortuna, for one. We think he's the one who killed your brother, though we have no proof of it."

"What makes you think it's him?"

"He has the most to gain. Brian seemed the most likely one to take your grandfather's place, but with him out of the way there's only you and one other brother, and that brother, Joey, has shown no interest at all in the family business."

"So you're saying," Adam concluded for her, "that I'm the only one who stands in Angelo's way?"

"I'm saying," she said softly, "that if I were you, I wouldn't turn my back on the man."

"Anything else?" Charlie asked.

"The other Eastern Seaboard families are getting nervous. They know that Salvatore is old and could die at any time. They know what to expect from Salvatore. He's always been a man of honor. His word is his bond. And if it's at all possible to avoid a confrontation, he'll find a way. But they don't know what to expect of you, Adam, or Angelo Fortuna. They're afraid of both of you." She looked at her boss. "And now, Charlie, I'd appreciate it if you'd tell me what's going on here."

"I'd be happy to. Mr. Danaro came here to discuss the case we're building against his grandfather and to ask us to lay off."

Tori looked curiously at her boss, trying to guess what was coming next. He knew how much time she'd spent sifting through decades' worth of information and piecing it together into something that could be used in court—even if it didn't amount to much. "And?" she prodded.

"And I've agreed to back away from the investigation for now."

Tori sat in stunned silence for a moment. "You what?"

"I said—"

"I know what you said." She glanced at the man standing near the window who looked calmly back at her. She addressed herself to her boss. "I'd like to speak with you."

"Go ahead."

"In your secretary's office."

He rose at the same time Tori did. "Excuse us, Mr. Danaro."

When they were in the hall, Tori turned on him. "What are you doing, Charlie? More than anyone else, you know how much time and effort I've put into getting together a case against Salvatore Danaro. Are you going to stand there and tell me it was all for nothing?"

"As far as getting him to court goes, yes."

"Yes?"

"Yes."

Tori paced for a moment and then stopped in front of her boss, pushing her hair away from her face. "You have good reasons for this, right?"

"I think so," he replied calmly.

"Would you care to share them with me?"

Charlie leaned against the edge of his secretary's desk. "Look, the old man is dying. I know it, he knows it and his grandson knows it. It's just a matter of time. Adam came here tonight to make a deal."

"A Danaro wants to make a deal?"

"You sound skeptical."

"Danaros don't make deals."

"They do if it means protecting their own. And Adam wants to make sure his grandfather's last days are as peaceful as possible."

Tori sat in his secretary's chair. "So what kind of deal are we talking about?"

"He's going to help us nail Angelo Fortuna."

Angelo Fortuna was a very dangerous man. "How? Why?"

"Which question do you want answered first?"

"The 'why' one."

"Because," came a deep voice from the doorway of Charlie's office, "Angelo Fortuna is responsible for my brother's death, a fact which you've just confirmed."

Tori turned her head and studied Adam Danaro's stony expression in the dim light. She wasn't going to be defensive with him anymore. She'd said she was sorry, and even though that wasn't nearly enough, it was all she could do. "I thought you people handled those things among yourselves. Vendetta, I believe you call it."

His eyes met hers. "Perhaps this is my way of handling the vendetta."

"And perhaps this is your way of getting us to back away from your grandfather until it's too late."

"There's no way you can be sure," he agreed expressionlessly.

Tori turned to her boss. "He's right. There's no way we can be sure. He might just be buying time."

Charlie nodded.

"And you're going to go along with this?" she asked in disbelief.

"I am. We have nothing to lose and everything to gain."

She shook her head. "This is unbelievable."

"Not really." Her boss smiled, obviously pleased with himself. "I have a plan."

He walked back into his office. Tori followed him, brushing against Adam as she passed him in the doorway. "Are you going to share this plan with me," she asked, "or leave me hanging here?"

Charlie smiled at her. "We're going to set Mr. Fortuna up."

"We?"

"Well, actually you. You and Mr. Danaro."

Tori looked at Adam, who still stood in the doorway, his arms folded across his chest.

"And where are you going to be while we're doing this?" she asked, turning back to Charlie.

"Right here." He patted his desk. "Taking your phone calls and telling you what to do."

"Contrary to what you might think, Parker, Fortuna isn't a stupid man," Adam said quietly.

"Believe me, I know that. But this plan is foolproof. You," he addressed Adam, "are going to dangle some of your grandfather's assets in front of Fortuna like a carrot before a rabbit. You're going to make him feel secure as though he actually has a chance at absorbing the Danaro family into his own. You are going to treat him like a friend and business partner."

"What does that have to do with nabbing him for murder?" Tori interrupted.

"Nothing."

"Nothing?" she echoed.

"We can't arrest him for murder because we have no eyewitness and I think the chance of his confessing is fairly slim."

"So?"

"So, we're going to get him for tax evasion," he informed her with satisfaction.

"Tax evasion?" Tori asked incredulously.

"Why are you repeating what I say this evening?"

"It's morning, and I'm repeating your words because I can't believe what I'm hearing."

"Trust me on this."

Tori turned to Adam who still stood quietly in the doorway, his arms folded across his chest. "What do you think?"

"I want Fortuna indicted for the murder of my brother."

"I know. I do, too," Charlie agreed, "but the fact is that we have no evidence, and even if we did he'd probably end up spending more time behind bars on the tax evasion charges than on a murder charge. Sad, but true."

Tori shook her head. "I still don't understand how we're going to catch him for tax evasion."

"It's simple. When he tries to produce enough assets to buy out the Danaro family's interests, we'll have him dead to rights. He makes a good piece of change with his import/export business and his chain of liquor stores, but nothing like what he'll need to buy out the Danaros."

"All right," Tori agreed. "That makes sense. But where do I come in?"

"You're going to work on the inside. I want you to watch what goes on and I want to be apprised of developments. You're going to be the agency's link with the Danaro family."

"But how?"

"You're going to live with him."

"Live with Adam?"

Charlie shook his head. "You're doing it again, Tori."

"I would never show my grandfather such disrespect by bringing a so-called girlfriend to live under his roof. No one in the family would," Adam calmly informed him. "And is there some reason why Miss Burton has to be the inside agent?"

"Because she knows the players, Danaro. If the two of you are a little uncomfortable with each other, that's too bad. You're just going to have to get over it. Now, if you can't bring her in as your girlfriend, how about as your wife?"

"Wi—" Tori caught herself and closed her mouth over the word.

"Wife," Charlie finished for her. "And if it seems a little sudden to some people, you can tell some story about your eyes meeting across a crowded room, etcetera, etcetera and so on and so forth. We'll arrange something here at the agency."

"No."

Tori and Charlie both turned to look at Adam. "Why not? As your wife she'd be able to come and go freely."

Adam's eyes rested on Tori. "I don't object to Victoria becoming my wife, in the business sense. It's the method I'm concerned about. If there's to be a marriage, it should be a real one in case someone decides to check on it."

"I could have the paperwork planted," Charlie told him.

"No." Adam was firm. "Just as you have your ways of finding things out, so do we."

Charlie nodded. "All right. We have marriage licenses here. You can use one of those."

Tori looked from one to the other. "Just a minute. Why do I have to go in as anyone's wife? What about as a nurse to Salvatore, or a housekeeper or something with a lower profile?"

"Because as his wife," Charlie explained, "you'll be expected to be involved more in your husband's affairs. You can't really meet his friends as a nurse or housekeeper. You wouldn't be able to attend social functions. When I say that I want you on the inside, I *mean* on the inside."

"But—"

"No 'buts.'" Charlie cut her off. "The game is set." He leaned back comfortably in his chair, his hands folded behind his head. "In summary, so we all understand what our obligations are, we'll drop our investigation of Salvatore and let the old man die in peace. In addition, we'll provide around-the-clock protection for the rest of his family, but in return for these favors you—" he looked at Adam "—will allow Tori into your home to work with you in gathering information against Angelo Fortuna for a tax case."

Tori didn't like it. All of her instincts told her this whole thing was doomed to failure, but she said nothing. Aside from the fact that Charlie wouldn't listen to her, she didn't want to show dissension in front of Adam.

Charlie rifled through a box full of index cards, stopped at one he liked, picked up the phone and dialed. There was a long wait before someone at the other end answered, which wasn't surprising, considering the time. "Hello," Charlie said, "I'd like to speak with Judge Martin Smith. This is Adam Danaro calling."

Adam lifted an expressive brow as he silently watched.

"Judge Smith?" Charlie continued after a moment's pause, "I have a favor to ask of you. I'm sorry for disturbing your sleep, and I certainly wouldn't do it if it wasn't an emergency, but my fiancée and I would like to get married tonight." He listened for a moment and nodded. "Yes, sir, I know, but a member of my family is gravely ill. I have to leave town immediately." Another pause while he listened. "Yes, sir, tonight." Charlie nodded. "We'll be there. And thank you."

He hung up and looked at them in satisfaction. "That's all taken care of. You two have an appointment with Judge Smith in exactly—" he looked at his watch "—one hour." He took the card out of the file and handed it to Tori. "This is his address."

She took it and looked up at Adam. The muscle in his jaw was taut, but that was the only visible sign of what he was feeling. He was selling his soul to buy his grandfather a little peace.

The phone buzzed and Charlie answered it, spoke a few words and hung up. "Remember to put on a good show for the judge. If anyone talks to him later, the last thing we want is for him to mention any odd behavior."

"And, of course, getting married at four in the morning is perfectly normal," Tori said dryly.

"For two people desperately in love it is," Charlie answered as he got to his feet, then took his jacket from a small closet. "And now, if you don't mind, I'm going home. It's been a long day. Lock up when you leave, Tori." He reached out to shake Adam's hand, but Adam didn't return the gesture and Charlie's hand fell awkwardly to his side. "Right. Well, good luck and be careful."

After Charlie had gone, Tori sat still, intensely aware of Adam's eyes on the back of her head. "I guess we should be going," she said. She rose and walked over to the coffee maker to shut it off.

"An FBI agent," Adam said as though she hadn't spoken. "Who would have guessed? You have such an innocent, all-American look about you."

Tori took a deep breath and met his look with a direct one of her own. "I've already said that I was sorry. If I'd known then what I know now, I never would have done it."

"Ah." He nodded. "Interesting. And exactly what was this revelation you apparently had?"

Her eyes searched his for any sign of the tenderness she'd once seen in them, and found none. How could she possibly make him understand that she'd fallen in

love with him? That was why she'd taken off the way
she had. When she'd made the arrangement to be
seated next to him on the overseas flight to Paris, her
intention had been simply to get to know the man who
was now the acting head of the Danaro family and, if
he turned out to be the boastful sort, perhaps find out
some things she didn't already know.

She'd known she was in trouble from the moment
their eyes had met. If she could have gotten off the jet
at that point, she would have. But it was too late.
Adam Danaro wasn't at all what she'd expected. He
had charm and wit and intelligence. He talked very
little about himself but asked Tori about her life and
her interests. Neither had watched the movie; neither
had slept. They'd spent the entire flight talking about
everything and anything.

And when they'd gotten to Paris, Tori intended to
turn around and come back home, but Adam invited
her out to dinner and she hadn't been able to refuse.
They spent one day together, walking around Paris,
talking, laughing, eating. And when he'd walked Tori
to her hotel room after dinner, he'd stood in the hallway with her, gently cupping her face and looking into
her eyes. "How is it that I lived through thirty-three
years without knowing you were somewhere in the
world as well?" he'd said.

Tori had always believed that one day she'd find the
man she was meant to be with—her other half. And
she knew as she stood in the hotel corridor with Adam
Danaro that he was it. But it was all wrong. There
wasn't any way they could ever be together by virtue

of who and what he was and who and what she was. It simply could never be.

She'd left Paris that night.

"Victoria?"

Adam's voice brought her back to the present. "Yes?"

"I asked if you want to go in my car or yours?"

"Oh. Yours will be fine, I suppose. The judge doesn't live too far from here. After the deed is done you can drop me off at my car."

He walked out of the office ahead of her. Tori turned out the lights and made sure the office door was locked. In silence they walked down a long hall, past a security guard who signed them out of the building and outside to where their cars were parked. Adam opened the passenger door of the black Porsche for her, then climbed into the driver's seat. The top was off, and as they drove through the quiet streets, the chilly fall air swirled around them, whipping Tori's hair. While they were at a stoplight, her gaze fell on Adam's hand as it gripped the stick shift. As soon as the light turned green he jammed it into first gear, then second and third and fourth. His angry movements contrasted oddly with the emotionless stone mask that had settled over his features.

"Turn right at the next corner," she said quietly as she came to an awareness of her surroundings. Her eyes went back to his hand, watching as he downshifted and smoothly made the turn.

They parked in front of the judge's home about ten minutes later. The lights were on. A woman opened the door and smiled at the two of them, seeming to be in amazingly good cheer considering the hour and the inconvenience. "My husband will be right with you," she told them as she led them into an elegant study, then left them alone, closing the doors after her.

Adam's eyes came to rest on Tori. "So, Agent Burton, do you do this often?"

"Do what?"

"Marry men you're not in love with? Or is that all in a day's work for you?"

His words stung. "I do what I have to to get the job done," she said quietly.

The judge walked in before they could say anything else. His white hair was a little mussed, as though he'd just awakened. He wasn't as cheerful as his wife as he motioned for the couple to stand before him. His wife and another woman stood off to the side to act as witnesses.

Tori's shoulder brushed against the man she was about to marry and she looked up at him only to find his eyes on her. What was he thinking? she wondered. It was impossible to tell.

The judge looked at them sternly over the rim of his glasses. "The union of two people in marriage is not something to be taken lightly," he began.

Tori lowered her eyes and looked at her clasped hands. She had to keep telling herself that this was just a job, like any other job, and one of these days it would be behind her. She only wished she'd had a little more time to mentally prepare herself. She had no way of knowing what she was walking into.

Adam suddenly reached over and took one of her hands in his, holding it firmly but lightly. He was surprised at how cool it was. She was obviously nervous, but it was impossible to tell that by simply looking at her composed features.

Just as Tori was about to repeat the vows, her husband-to-be interrupted. "One moment, Judge. It would appear that my fiancée is shy." He put his hand under her chin and raised her eyes to his. "That's better."

Tori took a deep breath and forced her eyes to remain on his as she repeated her vows, then stood silently and listened while Adam said his, their eyes locked as though in silent combat all the while. The judge smiled, seemingly pleased with himself. "You may kiss the bride."

Adam didn't noticeably hesitate as he cupped Tori's head in his hands and drew her mouth toward his. Her first very natural reaction was to resist, but his grip grew more firm, not allowing her that luxury and reminding her that people were watching. When their lips finally met, it was as though it were in slow motion, a contact she felt down to her toes. Anyone watching would have made the assumption that the two of them were already lovers. As Adam raised his head, his unamused eyes took in the heightened color of her cheeks. "An FBI agent who blushes," he said so softly only she could hear. "That has to be one for the record books."

The judge's wife approached at that moment and hugged Tori while the judge shook Adam's hand, and then stood with his arm around his wife. "We wish you both a long and happy life together."

Adam put his arm around Tori's shoulders and pulled her close to his side as they left, dropping it as soon as they were out of sight. Wordlessly, they made the drive back to where she worked. He parked alongside her car and sat there with the engine idling. He turned in his seat and looked at her. "I'm going back to Connecticut tonight, so how do you want to work this?"

Tori looked out the windshield. "I'll have to pack my things, and I'd like to bring my car. I think it would be best if I followed you tomorrow."

"Quite the professional, aren't you? Does anything ever crack that smooth facade of yours?"

Tori turned her head and met his gaze. "Why are you trying so hard to provoke me?"

"Is that how you perceive it?"

"I believe that's what my question implied."

"Let's just say I don't appreciate being blackmailed into cooperation with anyone."

"Blackmailed?"

"What would you call it? Either I cooperate or you make my grandfather's remaining days miserable."

"You're right." She surprised the man by agreeing with him, sounding none too proud of the fact. "But sometimes the end justifies the means."

The muscle in his jaw moved. "And sometimes," he said quietly, "it doesn't."

Tori's throat closed, making speech impossible. She wanted so badly to tell him how she felt, but she couldn't. He was so angry with her he would have thrown her words back in her face. Without saying anything, she opened the door and climbed out of the car.

"Victoria?"

She leaned back in.

The muscle in his jaw moved again as he looked at her. "I'll follow you home to make sure you get there all right. You shouldn't be out at this hour alone."

His sudden concern surprised her. "No, thank you," she said politely. "I'll be fine."

His eyes traveled over her, taking in the beautiful wavy hair and dark-lashed blue eyes set in creamy skin. "I'll follow you anyway."

"That's really not—" She stopped herself. If he wanted to make a nice gesture there was no reason she shouldn't accept it graciously. "Thank you."

She climbed into her car and started driving, intensely aware of who was behind the headlights reflected in her rearview mirror. The drive seemed to last forever.

When they finally arrived at her apartment building, Adam parked behind her and waited until she was inside before leaving. Tori went straight to her apartment. The phone was ringing as she let herself in, so she dropped her keys on the hall table and ran into her office to answer it. Charlie was on the other end of the line. "It's about time you got home. I've been calling you for half an hour."

"As you may or may not recall, I was getting married per your instructions." Her tone reflected her anger. "What were you trying to prove by having Adam in your office without warning me? You knew we'd met before."

"Sure, I knew you'd met. But I had a feeling there was more to that meeting than what you put in your report. From your display this evening, it would appear that I was right."

"The only things I didn't put in my report were those that didn't concern the agency."

"Everything concerns the agency."

"Is that what you called to tell me?"

"That's one reason I phoned. I didn't want to talk too much in front of Danaro."

Tori picked up a pencil and tapped the eraser on the desktop. "I'm listening."

"It's very simple. I don't want you to wait for whatever crumbs Danaro is willing to feed you. You are to make an active effort to gather information."

"On Angelo Fortuna," she clarified.

"And Adam Danaro."

Tori's pencil stopped in midair. "What?"

"We'll never get another chance like this. If Adam Danaro is in fact the head of the family, and I believe he is, he's the one we'll be going after next."

"But that wasn't part of the deal you made with him."

"That's right." Charlie was completely unapologetic. "We get these people any way we can, anytime we can."

"I don't like it."

"You're not paid to like it."

"Meaning what? You'll fire me if I don't do as I'm told."

There was a pause at the other end of the line. "No, nothing like that. Of course not."

"You made an agreement with Adam Danaro regarding Angelo Fortuna. He's going to let me live in his home because of this agreement and I, for one, am not going to sneak behind his back and try to dig up incriminating information about him."

"That's your final word?"

"That's right, Charlie."

"I hate it when you do that."

"Don't sulk. Your word should be worth something. You pull stuff like this and no one will trust you."

"It's just that it's such a marvelous opportunity..."

"That you hate to pass it up," she finished for him. "I know, and I'm sorry, but I just can't do it."

Charlie sighed. "All right. But even if you don't report everything to me, you keep your eyes and ears open for your own protection."

"What are you talking about?"

"Brian's murder wasn't a fluke. Someone wanted him dead. And someone might very well want Adam dead. I'd hate to see you get caught in the cross fire."

"Believe me, I'd hate that, too. It's nice of you to be concerned."

"I'm a nice guy."

"Right." Tori didn't sound convinced.

She could sense his smile. "Good night, Tori. Don't forget to call in when you get the chance. And from a pay phone, not the house phone."

After hanging up, Tori sat motionless for a long time in the semidark room, staring out of the window and watching the sun rise, a ribbon at a time, until the world outside was bathed in a soft orange glow. Who was it, she wondered, who'd said that "night was the morning's canvas"?

The thought went as quickly as it had come. She didn't feel good about this assignment. But more than that, she was uneasy. She was walking into a hostile world with no protection except for Adam, and he wasn't exactly thrilled with her at the moment. No one knew better than she what could happen to an FBI agent if he or she were so unlucky as to get caught by the men with whom she'd soon be mingling. It was a fate to be avoided at all costs.

With a tired sigh, she pushed her heavy hair away from her face and went into her bedroom to pack.

Chapter Two

The next evening, Tori stopped her white Fiat in front of a pair of tall wrought-iron gates and waited. Her heart was pounding a little harder than usual. She hated to attribute it to nerves, but that's definitely what it was. She'd always imagined that when she finally embarked on her first undercover assignment she'd have nerves of steel and instinctively know what to do every step of the way. It wasn't turning out that way at all. She was a wreck and she wasn't even inside the gates yet.

A pleasant-looking guard came out of a small brick and glass enclosure and approached her car. Tori rolled down the window and smiled at him. "Hello. My name is Victoria Burton. Excuse me," she said disarmingly, "I mean Victoria Danaro." The words sounded strange leaving her lips.

"Yes, ma'am," he said politely. "Mr. Danaro told me to expect you. Wait here for just a moment and I'll open the gates."

"Thank you." Tori sat there, drumming her fingers on the steering wheel. A moment later the gates opened silently and Tori passed through, stopping just a few feet past them. The Danaro compound spread out before her like a vast, well-tended park set right on Long Island Sound. It was breathtaking. Four sprawling stone houses set hundreds of yards apart were set among the trees.

The guard approached her car again. "Is there a problem, Mrs. Danaro?"

"I don't know which house to go to."

"First one."

"Thanks again." She put her car back in gear and heard the gravel from the drive crunch under her tires as she made her way to the house and parked. She leaned over the steering wheel and looked through the windshield at her new home. It was enormous, but not by any means unfriendly. In fact, if she hadn't known it belonged to Salvatore Danaro, she would have quite liked it.

Tori leaned back in her seat, took a deep breath and slowly exhaled. "All right," she told herself with calm determination—or rather a determination to be calm— "this is it. Dignity is the key word."

As she stepped out of her car, a large Irish setter ran over to her, barking loudly and wagging his tail. Tori hunkered down with a smile as she scratched his silky head. "Well, aren't you the ferocious watchdog?" His tail wagged even harder as he tried to lick her. As Tori laughed, her eyes alighted on a pair of men's shoes about ten feet away, then traveled up over dark pleated pants and a heavy white cable-knit sweater with an oxford shirt peaking out. Her smile faded as she found herself looking into Adam's dark brown eyes. So much for dignity, she thought as she straightened away from the dog. "Hello."

He just looked at her. "You're later than I expected."

"The traffic was heavy."

A woman about her own age suddenly came running out of the house and threw her arms around Tori. "You're here! I was afraid you wouldn't make it before I had to leave."

A corner of Adam's mouth lifted at Tori's look of helpless surprise. "Victoria, I'd like you to meet my sister, Caroline."

Caroline held Tori away from her and beamed. "I would never have believed my brother could do something this impulsive if I hadn't seen you for myself. Hearts the world over are breaking tonight."

Tori knew instantly that she was going to like this woman—even if she couldn't get a word in.

Caroline looked at her watch and clicked her tongue. "Damn, I'm late." She smiled at Tori. "But I'll be back the first chance I get and we'll have a nice long talk. And Adam—" she turned to her brother "—don't forget about the party I'm giving for the two of you Friday night." She hugged her brother and whispered loudly enough for Tori to hear, "She's lovely, Adam. Lovely."

Waving to both of them, Caroline climbed into her car and sped down the drive.

Tori watched until the car was out of sight, then turned to Adam. "Your sister's a real whirlwind."

"You'll like her when you get to know her."

"I already do."

Adam inclined his head toward the house. "Come on in."

Tori motioned toward the other houses. "Who lives in those?"

Adam looked down the drive. "Our family attorney and advisor, Sam Lange, lives in the house nearest us with his wife; the next house belonged to my brother Brian and his family." He was silent for a moment. "No one is there now. His wife and daughter went to live with her parents after Brian was killed."

"And in the last house?"

"We reserve that one for guests." He opened the front door for her and Tori found herself in a foyer that would have easily held twenty people. "Come on, Toby." Adam snapped his fingers and the Irish setter trotted quietly into the foyer and down the hall.

Adam placed his hand in the middle of Tori's back and guided her down the hall to a library/office where a fire took the chill out of the air. The view of the Sound from the huge window along one wall was exquisite, but it was the man in the room who held her attention. Adam waved her into a chair, then sat be-

hind his desk and looked at her, his elbows on the
chair arms, his fingers steepled under his chin, as he
leaned back, his eyes on hers. "I did some checking on
you."

She looked at him curiously. "Why?"

"Curiosity about the woman who was moving into
my home. Any objections?"

"No," she said quietly.

"I understand your father is a history professor."

"That's right."

"And your mother's been dead since you were
eight."

Tori nodded.

"Your father never remarried?"

"No. He raised me by himself."

"You must be very close."

"We are," she said quietly. "He's a very special
man."

Adam leaned forward and looked at a file that lay
open on his desk. "I see that he's also written some
books."

"Ten. Some are straight history texts, some are his-
torical novels."

"And you're listed as a researcher in all but two of
them."

"It's something I enjoy doing in my spare time."

His eyes rested on her with unnerving coolness. It
was all Tori could do to keep from shifting in her seat.

"If you've finished grilling me," she said without
any noticeable annoyance in her voice, "I'm a little

tired. I'd appreciate it if you'd show me to my room so I can unpack and rest for a little while."

Adam rose. "Where's your luggage?"

"In my car."

"Sesto!" he called out.

An enormous man, dressed in a suit, opened the door and looked in. "Yes, sir?"

"Please get my wife's luggage and bring it up to our room."

Tori glanced at Adam's profile, but waited until the bodyguard had gone before speaking. "Our room?"

Adam's eyes met hers, their expression unfathomable. "Anyone who knows me would realize that I'd never consent to having the woman I love sleeping in a separate room."

The woman he loved. "You're right, of course," she agreed. "I hadn't thought about it."

"Perhaps you should start thinking of these things. Neither of us can afford to be careless about appearances. It could cost both of us our lives."

He was right and she knew it. She had to remember that she was very much in enemy territory. She started to say something, but stopped when she saw the way he was looking at her. "What's wrong?"

Adam was silent for a moment. "Nothing," he finally said. "Come on, I'll show you to our room."

Tori followed him out of the library and up a long, winding staircase to the second floor. Adam opened a door at the end of the carpeted hallway and waited for Tori to precede him into the room. Her shoulder brushed against his chest as she passed him and she inhaled sharply, annoyed at the intensity of her reaction.

The room was very much a man's room, spacious but with very little furniture. The floor had wood around the perimeter, and cushioned gray carpeting in the middle. A large bed rested against one pearl-gray wall, a black modern-looking dresser against another. Two bookcases, both full, sat invitingly in a corner of the room. Tori walked over to the sliding glass doors that opened onto a balcony overlooking the grounds. "This is a wonderful room."

Adam looked around as though seeing it for the first time. "It's all right."

"Where should I put my things?"

"You can have half of the closet and I'm sure there're some empty drawers."

"Thank you." Her eyes searched the room. "My luggage isn't here yet."

"That's all right. I'd like to introduce you to my grandfather before you do anything else anyway."

"Does he know about us?"

"No. I told him that I met you in Paris last year, we'd lost touch, and when we met again in Washington, realized we were in love and got married. I don't want him to know the truth."

"I won't say anything."

"Thank you."

"Do you think he's going to suspect anything when he realizes the agency isn't bothering him anymore?"

"What he might suspect and what he knows are two different things. Understand?"

"Yes."

"Come on." He put his hand in the middle of her back and steered her out of the bedroom and down the hall.

The door was open and the first thing Tori saw was an old man sitting up in bed, leaning against some pillows. So, this was Salvatore Danaro, she thought almost in awe. He smiled when he saw her and Tori returned his smile.

"Grandfather," Adam said as he walked her into the room, "this is my wife, Victoria."

The old man took both of her hands in his and looked her over with tired but intelligent eyes. "She's beautiful," he told his grandson, his eyes still on her. "Absolutely beautiful."

Adam gazed intently at her profile and then away. "I know."

"Sit, please," he addressed Tori. "Let's get to know each other."

Adam pulled out a chair for her next to the bed. As Tori sat down, she looked up into Adam's eyes and wondered what he was thinking. It was impossible to tell.

"So, young lady, tell me, how many children do you and my grandson plan to have?"

It wasn't the question she'd been expecting. "How many children?" She looked at Adam. "Would you like to field this one?"

Adam didn't smile. "We haven't discussed starting a family yet, Grandfather."

Salvatore looked from one to the other. "I see. Don't you think maybe you should?"

Adam looked at his watch. "I'm sure we'll get around to it eventually."

"I don't mean to sound pushy," Salvatore continued, "but you should start your family planning now. Besides," he said with a smile, "I'd love to see my great-grandchild before I die."

Adam looked at his watch again. "I have to make a phone call."

Salvatore smiled at Tori. "Since your husband's going to be otherwise occupied, perhaps you could sit with me for a while."

Tori looked at Adam and Salvatore looked at both of them. "Unless," he continued, "you have other things to do."

"Oh, no," Tori answered. "I'm really quite free."

"Good. I'd like you to read to me with that delightful voice of yours."

Tori wasn't quite sure what she'd expected Salvatore to be like, but this certainly wasn't it. He was charming. "I'd like that very much. That is—" she glanced toward Adam "—if it's all right with you."

He looked back at her and she got the distinct impression he wasn't pleased with leaving her behind. Perhaps he was afraid she'd ask too many questions. "Not for too long. Victoria hasn't even had time to unpack."

Tori stared at the empty doorway long after Adam had passed through it. This was definitely going to be one of her more difficult assignments.

"Victoria?"

She turned back to Salvatore and forced a smile to her lips.

"Is something wrong?"

"Oh, no, not really."

Salvatore looked at her skeptically. "I may be old, but I'm still observant."

Tori decided to be as honest as she dared. "It's just that I don't know Adam very well and sometimes I don't understand him."

"Oh." He nodded. "That's nothing to worry about. The understanding will come with time."

"I'm sure it will."

"Adam tells me that you two met on an airplane to Paris."

"That's right."

"I knew when he came back from that trip that something had happened."

"How?"

"He was different. Distracted. I've known Adam all of his life, and I can't recall ever seeing him distracted before. But now that I've met you, I understand completely."

"Are you sure you're not Irish?" she asked suspiciously.

"You think I'm full of blarney?"

"I think you've at least kissed the stone."

Salvatore smiled tiredly. "We Italians have our share of charm, you know."

"I'm learning."

The old man shook his head and grew more serious. "Seeing you and Adam together reminds me of how much I miss my Katherine."

"Your wife?"

"My beautiful wife."

"How long ago did she die?"

"It's been almost twenty years, but it still hurts."

Tori sympathetically covered his hand with hers. "I'm truly sorry, Mr. Danaro."

"Please, call me Salvatore," he told her as he patted her hand and smiled gently. "What are you thinking behind those beautiful blue eyes of yours, Victoria Danaro?"

"That you're a very nice man," she said honestly, a note of surprise in her voice.

"There are those who would strongly disagree with you, dear."

"Aren't there always?"

Salvatore's smile grew. "I think I like you. I think I like you very much. My grandson chose wisely."

She let that pass, but the old man looking at her saw a shadow pass over her expression. "What would you like me to read?" she asked in an effort to change the conversation.

He indicated a book on the bedside. "*Tom Sawyer.*"

Tori picked up the book and looked at the binding in pleasant surprise. "I haven't read that for years."

"Neither have I. And there are other books I can remember loving when I was young that I want to read while I recover."

Tori looked quickly at him but said nothing. From what she understood of his heart condition, he would never recover. She opened the book to the marked page, then looked back at Salvatore. "May I get you anything before we start?"

He looked suddenly very tired and very old as he settled himself down into the bed and relaxed against the pillow. "No, thank you. I'm quite content at the moment."

Tori watched him. It was so hard to associate this nice, articulate man with what she knew of his history. By all accounts he was a gentleman, but a mobster was a mobster was a mobster, no matter how one colored it. She turned her attention to the book and read quietly for nearly half an hour, until she was sure he was asleep. With great care, she closed the book and set it back on the bedside table. He looked so helpless lying there that Tori felt a twinge of guilt. More than a twinge. All of the work she'd done over the past two years to put him in prison suddenly didn't seem very important. Perhaps it was best this way. Not the deception, but the idea of getting Angelo Fortuna rather than Salvatore Danaro was becoming more appealing all the time.

She got up and walked across the room making as little noise as possible and quietly closed the door behind her.

A woman in a white nurse's uniform was standing just outside. "Hi," she whispered. "I'm Linda."

"Hello," Tori whispered back, extending her hand. "Victoria Danaro."

"Nice to meet you. I was just in the kitchen, and I got the distinct impression that you should make a special effort to introduce yourself to Mrs. Rosetti."

"Mrs. Rosetti?"

"The cook and housekeeper. She's been with the family for more than thirty years and rules things around here with an iron hand."

"I didn't know that."

"So like I said, I think you should go down and introduce yourself."

"Thank you for the warning. I'll do it."

"Excuse me, but I'd better be getting back to work. Maybe we can have a cup of coffee together later." Linda walked past her and went into Salvatore's room.

Tori started to go to her own room to unpack, but decided instead to go to the kitchen to meet the fearsome Mrs. Rosetti. The kitchen was easy enough to find. She just followed the hallway from the bottom of the stairs to its logical conclusion and there it was. She pushed open the swinging door and looked in. Standing at an island in the middle of the sparkling and modern room and wielding a big wooden spoon in a kettle from which delicious aromas wafted, was a woman who could only be Mrs. Rosetti. Her iron-gray hair was braided and wrapped around her head. She wore a black dress with no white to give it relief, and she appeared to thoroughly enjoy her own cooking.

"Mrs. Rosetti?"

The woman turned and looked at her.

"I'm Adam's wife, Victoria."

She broke into a smile. "Of course, of course. Come in, dear, come in." She tapped the spoon on the edge of the pot and set it down, then wiped her hands off on the dark apron that was tied around her ample waist before engulfing Tori in her arms. "I can't believe it. When Mr. Danaro told me that Adam had gotten married I was in shock for at least an hour." She held Tori away from her and shook her head. "And look at you. Just look at how lovely you are."

"Mrs. Rosetti, have you seen—" Adam stopped in the doorway and looked at the two of them "—my wife."

"I certainly have." She gave Tori a last hug and let her go. "And now that you're both here, I want to tell you that in honor of the occasion, I'm fixing a special dinner tonight. Candlelight, wine, everything. But if I'm going to get anything done, I need some peace and quiet." She shooed them toward the door as she shook her head. "Though why you should be spending your first night together here I'll never know. You should be on a honeymoon. Young people today—everything is hurry, hurry, hurry. But who am I to say?" she muttered more to herself than to them. "I'm just the cook. I mind my own business." Then she noticed that they were still standing there watching her, and she picked up her wooden spoon and waved it at them. "Go. Go on, now."

Adam walked over to the cook and kissed her on the cheek. "Thank you, Mrs. Rosetti. I appreciate the sentiment, but I might not be back in time for dinner tonight."

The cook turned shocked eyes on him. "You might not be here on your bride's first night under your roof? You should be ashamed of yourself." She muttered something in Italian. "I'll tell you what," she spoke again in English. "I'm going to fix this dinner anyway, and I'm going to serve it in the living room in front of the fireplace, and you, young man, better show up or I'll want to know why in the morning." Then she turned to Tori. "Start out as you mean to go on. If you let him get away with this now, it'll only get worse. I know."

Tori obligingly turned to her husband. "Adam, I'd like you to come to dinner tonight if it's at all possible."

Mrs. Rosetti rolled her eyes. "Oh, that's telling him." Again she shook her head and muttered in Italian.

Adam guided Tori from the kitchen to the foot of the stairs with an impersonal hand in the middle of her back. "Your luggage is in your room now. You might as well unpack. I'll see you when I see you." He turned to go, but Tori's voice stopped him.

"May I ask where you're going?"

His eyes raked coldly over her. "You may ask anything you want, but don't necessarily expect an answer. You're here for a specific purpose. I have no intention of filing a log of my movements with you or anyone else."

"Of course. I'm sorry." She was on the first step, which made her eye level with Adam. "It wasn't my intention to pry. I don't really even know why I asked."

He inclined his dark head in acknowledgement of her apology and turned to leave, but stopped again. "I'll try to make it for dinner, Victoria," he said with his back to her.

"Thank you," she said quietly. "It obviously means a lot to Mrs. Rosetti."

He looked at Sesto, who was standing near the library door, and made a barely perceptible movement with his head before walking down the hall. Sesto followed immediately.

Deep in thought, Tori climbed the stairs to her room where she found her luggage waiting for her. Taking her time, she carefully unpacked and put things away, saving her gun for last. She searched the room for a safe place to put her Walther PPK, finally storing the gun on an upper shelf of the closet and the bullet clip in the pocket of one of her jackets. She hadn't liked guns before joining the FBI and now, even after all of the training she'd had with them, she still didn't like them.

Tori started to close the closet door, but stopped and looked at Adam's things. After just a slight hesitation, she reached out and ran her fingers over the cool cotton of his shirts. Taking one of his jackets off its hanger, she draped it across her shoulders and stepped onto the balcony, her arms crossed over her breasts to hold the jacket in place. It was already dark outside. The wind had picked up and was blowing dry leaves into a frenzy all over the compound. As Tori stood there, deep in thought, she unconsciously rubbed her cheek against the rough material of the jacket and smiled. It smelled just like Adam. Clean.

It took a moment for her to become aware of the knocking. Stepping into the room, she listened carefully. The knock came again.

"Mrs. Danaro?"

Tori crossed the room and opened the door to find Mrs. Rosetti standing there.

"I just wanted to tell you that your dinner's ready." She unsuccessfully tried to look past Tori without being obvious.

Tori looked at her watch in surprise. "Is it eight-thirty already? I hadn't realized." Then she looked at the cook apologetically. "I'm sorry, but Adam isn't back yet."

Mrs. Rosetti's mouth tightened. "Well, there's no sense in your starving yourself. Come downstairs and I'll serve you."

Tori followed her down the stairs and into the living room. A small table covered with a starched white cloth sat near a fire, which gave the room its only light except for the single candle in the middle of the table. "Oh, Mrs. Rosetti," she said appreciatively, "this is just beautiful."

The cook clicked her tongue in disapproval as she went to the kitchen and returned a few moments later with a plate full of pasta and a fresh green salad. "Here you go, dear." She patted Tori's shoulder sympathetically. "You might as well have some wine," Mrs. Rosetti told her as she picked up a bottle from the table and filled Tori's glass. "And if you won't be needing me anymore tonight, I think I'll clean up the kitchen and go home."

"Don't you live here?" Tori asked as she took her seat and spread the white linen napkin on her lap.

"No. My husband and I live a few miles away from the compound." She touched Tori's shoulder again. "I'm so sorry, dear. Men can be amazingly thoughtless."

Tori felt compelled to defend the absent Adam. "Mrs. Rosetti, I know he would have been here if it had been at all possible."

"Humpf." Without saying anything else, she turned and walked from the room.

Tori spent the next ten minutes picking at her food. It looked delicious, but she wasn't very hungry. Finally giving up, she picked up her wineglass and carried it over to the couch where she sat with her legs curled under her, staring at the fire. Every few minutes she looked at her watch, and the later it got the more worried she grew. When it got to be midnight, Tori decided to give up the vigil. If he was all right, he'd come home when he could. If he wasn't all right, there was nothing she could do about it.

When she got to her room, she washed her face and brushed her teeth, then slipped into a full, old-fashioned white cotton nightgown. Standing in front of the mirror, she brushed her hair with long strokes, her eyes glued to her reflection without really seeing it. But suddenly she focused. Her hand stopped in mid-stroke as Tori stared at her face as though seeing it for the first time. What did Adam see when he looked at her? Did she even want to know? At the moment her eyes seemed larger than usual, and just a little lost. Her dark lashes lent a smoky effect to her blue eyes. Her face was pale, as though she hadn't been in the sun much lately—which she hadn't. Her thick, dark mane of hair was considered unmanageable when she was younger, but in the world of today's fashion was effortlessly stylish.

As she looked at the overall picture, she knew that something was missing, but she couldn't quite put her finger on it. She set the brush down and with her palms flat on the dresser, leaned closer to the mirror and looked into her eyes. Suddenly she knew. There had once been a vivid sparkle in her eyes that she couldn't find now. When had it disappeared? She knew the answer. The night she'd left Paris. The night she'd left Adam Danaro.

Tori lowered her eyes, unable to bear the sight of herself any longer. Climbing into bed with a sigh that came from her heart, Tori reached over and turned out the bedside lamp, then lay absolutely motionless as she stared at the ceiling in the dark room.

Adam Danaro. His name and image were permanently engraved in her thoughts. Intellectually she'd known from the time she'd met him that there could never be anything between them, but her heart didn't always listen to her mind—a character flaw she'd spent years trying unsuccessfully to change.

She turned her head and looked at the empty pillow next to hers, and without her realizing it, a tear

slipped from the corner of her eye. Tori slowly closed
her eyes and turned her face toward the wall.

Adam walked into the dark bedroom and flipped a
switch that turned on the dresser lamp. He was
halfway into the room when he noticed Tori asleep in
bed. Tossing his sport coat over the back of a chair, he
went into the bathroom and splashed cold water on his
face, then stood with his hands on the sides of the ba-
sin, staring down at the black porcelain but not really
seeing it. After a moment, he straightened, wiped his
face off with a towel and went back into the bedroom. Tori was still sleeping. Adam walked to the bed
and stood looking down at her, his jaw taut but his
expression unfathomable. With a surprisingly gentle
hand, he reached out and pushed her hair away from
her face.

Tiredly rubbing his forehead, he crossed the room
and turned out the light, then sank into a chair about
ten feet away from the bed and sat there in absolute
stillness, his eyes on Tori.

Chapter Three

Tori lay very still in the big bed, waking slowly, becoming gradually aware of her surroundings. When she finally opened her eyes, a dim light filtered into the room as though it was very early in the morning. Turning her head, she saw that the drapes were closed and the light was coming in through a small open space in the middle. When she'd gone to bed last night, the drapes had been open, which meant that someone else had come in and closed them. Adam. Then she noticed that the other side of the bed had been slept in. So he *had* come home last night.

Suddenly the bathroom door opened and Adam stepped out, his hair still wet from the shower, a towel slung casually around his neck and another riding low on his hips. Her eyes trailed over his well-defined, flat stomach to his broad shoulders. Even standing as he was with his arms at his sides, she could see the curve of his biceps. Until this moment she'd never even seen him without a shirt, and she found she liked his leanly muscled body.

As he towel dried his hair, Adam glanced toward the bed and saw that she was awake. "Morning."

She pulled her sheet a little higher without even realizing what she was doing. "Good morning."

"Did you sleep all right?" he asked as he walked to the drapes and drew them open, allowing a flood of sunlight in.

"Just fine. I didn't even hear you come in."

"I know." He went to his closet and pulled out a white shirt with a narrow charcoal stripe in it and a pair of pleated charcoal trousers. Tori watched the muscles of his back as he moved. "Sorry I didn't make it back for dinner."

She tore her eyes from his body. "Oh, I didn't mind. It's Mrs. Rosetti you need to apologize to."

"She didn't take it well?"

"Let me put it this way: If I were you, I'd strongly consider going out for breakfast this morning."

"Point taken." He went back into the bathroom and Tori heard the hum of an electric razor. It was such a strangely intimate noise. He emerged a few minutes later with his clothes on, buttoning his shirt.

Tori looked at Adam's side of the bed and then at Adam. "I noticed that you slept with me last night."

His eyes held hers. "I didn't sleep *with* you, Victoria," he said evenly. "I slept next to you. A small but important distinction."

Tori didn't say anything. In fact, she wished she'd never brought it up in the first place.

"Is that a problem for you?" he asked as he knotted his tie and tightened it around his neck.

She made herself look him in the eye. "No. I was just surprised. I thought maybe you'd sleep on . . ."

"The floor?" he finished for her.

"Something like that."

"Victoria, we're both grown-ups. It's a big bed and you don't take up much space in it. There's no reason for either of us to sleep elsewhere. I realize you don't have a lot of confidence in my character, but I assure you that I'm not in the habit of forcing myself onto unwilling women."

"Please don't put words in my mouth. I never said anything about your character."

"Some things don't need to be verbalized to be understood."

Tori was silent for a moment, afraid that if she spoke her wavering voice would betray her. "I shouldn't have said anything about your sleeping in the bed," she finally managed.

Adam looked down at her and sighed. "I'm the one who's sorry, Victoria. I've been on edge ever since you showed up. I'll work on it. This has to be as distasteful to you as it is to me."

His words stung, even though that wasn't his intention.

"So," he said conversationally, "have you ever done anything like this before?"

"Like what?"

"Working undercover."

Tori couldn't stop the irrepressible dimple that suddenly creased her cheek. "Well, not *this* far undercover."

For the first time since she had seen him in Paris, Adam smiled at her. It was just a flash of white, gone as quickly as it had come, but it was a smile. His dark eyes rested on her. "Why don't you get up and come downstairs with me? Help me face Mrs. Rosetti. I don't think I can do it alone and on an empty stomach."

Tori looked at him curiously. "Why are you being so civil to me?"

Adam moved closer to the bed. He reached out and lifted a handful of her hair and let it fall through his fingers, then trailed the back of his fingers down her still warm, sleep-flushed cheeks. "Because at the moment, with your hair mussed and no makeup, you look like a vulnerable child." His eyes looked into hers with such intensity that it took her breath away.

Suddenly his hand fell to his side. "Do you want me to turn my back?"

Tori pushed her intense physical and emotional reaction to this man as far away from her as she could. "No, thank you," she answered without looking at him. Flipping the sheet down, she got to her feet and crossed the room to the closet. "I daresay you've seen women in things a lot more revealing than this."

Adam watched her as she got her clothes and went into the bathroom. When he heard her turn on the shower a moment later, he walked onto the balcony and stared out over the grounds. He didn't want her here, but he had no choice. He'd gone over all of the options last night and none was workable. If she left they'd start on his grandfather again. But if they thought he was going to let Angelo Fortuna get nailed for tax evasion rather than murder, they had underestimated him.

"Adam?" Tori said from the doorway. "I'm ready."

He turned and looked at her. She had on a khaki-colored full skirt, a bright yellow blouse and a wide khaki and yellow belt at her small waist. She stood with her hands in her skirt pockets looking at him as he looked at her.

"Is something wrong?"

Brown eyes met blue as a corner of his mouth lifted. "Let's face the dragon," he said without answering her.

When they got to the kitchen, Mrs. Rosetti greeted Tori with warmth, but a cool breeze definitely crossed over Adam. "Well," she said as she buttered some toast and put it on a tray, "I'm glad to see you can at least make it to breakfast with your wife. She had her first dinner in her new home alone." She poured juice into a small glass and set that on the tray as well. "I mind my own business. Anyone who knows me knows that I mind my own business, but that's shoddy treatment by anyone's standards and I can't in good conscience hold my tongue. Your poor bride was nearly in tears."

Adam looked curiously at Tori and Tori lifted her shoulders.

"I'm sorry, Mrs. Rosetti," Adam apologized. "It couldn't be helped."

"And I suppose you're going to be too busy Friday night to come to the party your sister's having for you?"

"Victoria and I will be there."

"Here."

"Excuse me?"

"She's having it here. Her apartment's too small."

"Then Victoria and I will both be here."

Mrs. Rosetti picked up the tray. "I'm going to take this to your grandfather. I'll be back in a moment to prepare your breakfasts."

"I'd be happy to do it," Tori offered.

"Thank you, but no. That's my job, dear. You just relax."

Adam handed Tori half of the newspaper after the cook had gone. "I think you've made a friend for life in Mrs. Rosetti."

"I'm sure I made a rather pathetic picture alone at the table last night. Sorry about that."

"You have nothing to be sorry about. I was the one who wasn't here."

Where were you? she wondered to herself. "What are we going to be doing today?" she asked aloud.

"I have some meetings, but nothing that concerns you."

"What about Angelo?"

"What about him?"

Tori lowered her voice. "He's why I'm here. Are you trying to set up any kind of meeting with him?"

"Even if I was, you wouldn't be able to attend."

"Why not?"

"Because things aren't done that way."

"But . . ."

"Stop grilling me, Victoria. When I have some information to give you, I'll do just that."

She looked at him, puzzled. There was something about his tone. "You never had any intention of cooperating, did you?"

"Let's just say that things aren't going to go exactly the way you and your agency think they will, but that you'll still get your man in the end."

"We agreed on a certain procedure. . . ."

His dark eyes bored into her. "We did no such thing. Your boss seemed to think it was important to have an agent here, so you're here. But keep in mind that you're on my turf now, Agent Burton, and you'll do things my way, or not at all."

"Adam, you can't do this."

His mouth twisted slightly into a cynical smile. "Watch me."

Linda, Salvatore's nurse, walked in at that moment wearing her coat and carrying her purse. She smiled at the couple but focused on Tori. "Mr. Danaro would like to see you when you have a moment."

It was several seconds before Tori could tear her angry eyes from Adam. "It would appear that I have one right now." She started to rise, but Adam caught her arm. Tori looked down at where he was holding her and then at him. "Take your hand off me."

Without taking his eyes from Tori, Adam spoke to the nurse. "Wait outside the kitchen."

The nurse looked from one to the other and quietly left the room.

As soon as she'd gone, Adam took his hand from Tori's arm. "You haven't had breakfast yet."

"I've lost my appetite."

"For food perhaps, but not for battle."

"You're the one who created a war zone, Adam, not me."

"It's not a war zone, Victoria, but the lines have been drawn," he said coolly.

"There are ways around your lines."

"I would suggest that you not try to find them if you value your life."

"Is that a threat?"

"I don't threaten. If you'd done your homework over the past two years as your boss claimed, you'd know that."

"No, I wouldn't," Tori said softly. "All I knew about you when I got on that plane were facts on paper: where you went to school; what kind of work you did before coming back into the family; the women you knew and the company you kept."

Adam leaned back in his chair and studied her. "I see. So tell me, Victoria, what did you learn about me in Paris that you didn't find in your files?"

Tori said nothing. She was afraid her voice would waver and give her away.

"Shall I tell you what I learned?" he asked emotionlessly. "That you can't be trusted." He leaned forward, his eyes on hers. "You are here because I have no choice in the matter and that's the only reason. And as soon as I can get you out of here, you'll be gone. I don't want you bothering my grandfather or pumping him for information and I don't want you getting friendly with the rest of my family. They deserve better than this little charade."

Tori swallowed hard. She was hurt and angered by his words. "I understand. But as you said, I'm not to be trusted so if I was you, I'd have me watched." She started to leave, but turned back. "You know, Adam, I'm not here by choice. I want nothing better than to get out of your life and to get you out of mine, but that's not going to happen until Angelo Fortuna is indicted. By cooperating with me, you just might get me out of here sooner. Think about it."

As Tori was leaving the kitchen, Mrs. Rosetti was coming back in. She looked from Tori to Adam and realized that they weren't going to have breakfast together, then shook her head. "Young people today," she muttered. Tori started to say something, but Mrs. Rosetti raised her hand. "I know. You're sorry." She crossed the kitchen and slammed a skillet onto the stove. "I don't know why the two of you bothered to get married in the first place. A long-distance call now and then would serve the same purpose. But it's none of my business. I'm not going to interfere."

Adam's dark eyes followed Tori out of the kitchen. As soon as the door had swung shut behind her, he slammed his newspaper onto the table and swore softly under his breath, oblivious to Mrs. Rosetti watching from the stove.

Tori stood outside the closed door and took a deep breath. Why was she torturing herself over this man? She was nothing to him. Less than nothing.

"Are you all right?" the nurse asked.

Tori inhaled sharply. She'd forgotten about Linda. It took a moment, but she managed a smile. "I'm fine."

Linda patted her arm. "Arguments are tough, I know, but chin up, it'll all blow over. They always do."

Not this one, Tori thought. Never this one. "Do you know what Mr. Danaro wants to see me about?" Tori asked, changing the subject.

Linda stopped at the bottom of the staircase. "I think he just likes your company," she said as she buttoned up her coat. "I'm going out for a short time, but I should be back within the hour."

"Is there anything I should know? Anything I can do for him while you're gone?"

"Just be patient. I think Mr. Danaro is used to a lot of activity, and he's finding his limitations since the heart attack very frustrating."

Tori stood there for a moment after the nurse left and tried to get her bearings. As she stared at the kitchen door, Adam walked through it. He stopped when he saw her and the two of them just stood there looking at one another. Tori's eyes fell first. Very quietly, she turned and climbed the stairs to Salvatore's room, aware of Adam's eyes on her back. She found Salvatore sitting in a wheelchair near the window.

He smiled when he saw her. "Ah, Victoria, how nice of you to come up so quickly. I hope I didn't take you away from anything important."

"Not at all."

"I thought maybe you could take an old man for a walk."

"If you're the man in question, I'd like that very much."

He smiled at her diplomatic omission of the word old. "I am. It's a great day out and I want to be part of it."

"What about your breakfast?" She'd noticed the tray that Mrs. Rosetti had fixed earlier was sitting on a table near his chair and was virtually untouched.

"It's kind of hard to work up an appetite when all you do is sit and sleep. Maybe the fresh air will make me hungry."

"So you'll eat when we get back?"

"I promise."

"Then let's go."

"Get my sweater, will you? It's in the top drawer of the dresser."

She did, and took a folded blanket from the foot of his bed. The day might well be beautiful, but it was still fall.

"Are you going to be warm enough in that?" he asked looking at her skirt and blouse.

"It's heavier than it looks." She put the blanket on his lap and turned the wheelchair around. "How do I go about getting you downstairs?"

"The elevator. Turn left as you go out the door."

She did, and sure enough a wrought-iron elevator that looked several decades old stood open and ready. She wheeled him into it and closed the well-oiled doors by hand. There were no floor buttons. Simply arrows pointing up and down. She pressed the down arrow and the elevator descended slowly.

When they finally stopped, she opened the wrought-iron gates and pushed the wheelchair through them into the foyer.

Sesto, who was sitting there in a chair reading a newspaper, rose abruptly and opened the door for them. "Thank you, Sesto," Salvatore said with a smile. "How's that nice wife of yours?"

"Fine, Mr. Danaro, just fine."

"And your new son?"

"Getting bigger all the time."

Tori maneuvered the wheelchair down a ramp that had been set up next to the stairs, stopped for a moment and looked around. "Is there any particular place you'd like to go?" she asked.

"By the water. I've missed listening to it lately. That nurse won't let me leave my window open."

Tori obediently pushed the chair across the lawn to a sunny spot on the bank of the Sound. She saw a boathouse and several docks that she hadn't been able to see from the window of her room.

"Turn me to face the sun, Victoria."

She did, and unfolded the blanket across his lap and spread it completely over him. "How's that?"

"Perfect." He looked at her from the corner of his eye. "Victoria seems very formal. What do your friends call you?"

"Tori."

"Tori," he said thoughtfully, "I like that. I think I'll use it."

There was no asking permission for this man, she thought with a smile.

"What does my grandson call you?"

She looked at him curiously. "Victoria. Why?"

"Just interested."

Tori sat on a white bench and watched as Salvatore settled back into his chair and raised his face to the warmth of the sun. When he seemed to be resting comfortably, she let her eyes wander around the grounds. This was a wonderful place. She would have loved being here were the circumstances different. And what a wonderful place for children to be raised. There was so much for them to do during the summer. It was sort of like having your own camp right outside your back door.

"Tori," Salvatore said after about half an hour, "you're a very restful woman to be around. You know when not to talk."

"Wait until you get to know me better," she said with a smile. "Would you like to go back to the house now?"

He adjusted the blanket. "In a few more minutes. This is so nice I hate to go back inside."

A man in a suit coat walked by, a walkie-talkie in his hand, obviously patrolling the grounds. The wind blew his jacket open and she saw a gun in a shoulder holster. Another suited man cruised slowly by in a motorboat. There was certainly no lack of security around the compound.

Salvatore had been watching Tori without her realizing it. "Don't let them make you nervous," he reassured her. "We've never had any trouble here, but I've always felt that it's better to be safe than sorry."

"I wasn't nervous. I was just wondering why all that security is necessary."

He nodded, a faraway look in his eyes. "Back in the old days it wasn't. No one would ever bother you in your home where innocent women and children might be harmed."

"Times have changed," she said quietly.

"Times have changed," he repeated softly, "and not for the better. Today there is little honor. Profit is everything. Everything and nothing. All of the old guard is dead. Gianini. Baldassare. Christiano. All gone."

Tori listened in fascination as he listed some of the biggest names in the history of organized crime.

"As the names have changed, so have the rules. It used to be man against man. If someone cheated or betrayed you, justice was swift and sure. An eye for an eye. But with the new breed coming up today, honor is a thing of the past. Wives and children are dragged into it." He shook his white head. "Things are out of control, Tori. It's time to end the madness."

She looked at him, wondering what he was talking about. "How?"

"That, my dear, I'm not at liberty to discuss." He glanced at Tori and sighed. "Listen to me talking to you like this. I think that heart attack affected my brain."

She saw a movement from the corner of her eye and looked in the direction of the house. Adam was crossing the lawn and walking toward them. As he drew closer, Tori looked at his face. Something was obviously wrong.

"Hello, Victoria." He stopped in front of her.

"Hello, Adam."

"You can go on back to the house. I'll see that my grandfather returns safely to his room in a few minutes."

She was obviously being dismissed, and she didn't dare argue with him about it in front of Salvatore. "All right," she said as she rose. "I'll see if I can help someone around the house."

"You aren't here to clean, Victoria," Adam said quietly. "Relax and read a book if you feel like it. There's no need to feel guilty about not having anything to do."

A half smile touched her mouth. "I'll try to remember that." She started to walk away, but Adam's voice stopped her.

"And Victoria? If you decide to leave the grounds, I want to know about it beforehand."

A curious frown creased her forehead. "All right. May I ask why?"

"Just do as I say."

Salvatore watched the two of them with growing interest. When Tori finally walked away, he turned his dark gaze onto his grandson. "What's going on between the two of you?"

Adam took his eyes from Tori's disappearing back. "What do you mean?"

"I see the way you look at her and I see the way she looks at you. There's no denying that the two of you are in love, but there's so much anger and hurt that goes along with it."

Adam said nothing.

"You never greet each other with a hug or kiss."

"I don't like public displays of affection."

"I'm not public, I'm family, and I want to know what's going on. I know the two of you are really married because I had it checked out. What I want to understand is why you're the way you are with each other."

Adam looked back toward the house just as Tori was disappearing inside. "Let's just say that Victoria and I have some problems to work out."

"Then you should have done that before the marriage."

"I agree. We made a mistake."

Salvatore shook his head. "I know you, Adam. You wouldn't make a mistake like that. You've got the right woman, but something is going on between the two of you. I want to help you if I can."

"I appreciate that, but you can't."

"Is she upset about your role in the family?"

"She's upset about a lot of things. So am I."

"Adam," he said quietly, "listen to an old man. That girl you married is someone very special. Don't let your pride ruin what's between you because if you do, you'll regret it for the rest of your life."

Adam tiredly dragged his fingers through his hair. "It's not that simple."

"Nothing between a man and a woman in love is simple. If it was, life would be boring."

"Not with Victoria," Adam said softly, looking toward the house. "Never with Victoria."

"So you do love her."

Adam met his grandfather's look with a direct one of his own. "I love her. And I want her out of here. I want her where she'll be safe."

"If it's a matter of..."

"It's a matter of honor, grandfather. Something you understand as well as anyone can."

"Then send her away."

"I can't do that."

"Because she's an FBI agent?"

Adam looked at him sharply but said nothing.

"As I said before," Salvatore told him, looking inordinately pleased with himself, "I did a little checking. It was an easy fact to discover."

"How easy?"

"Three phone calls."

Adam shook his head. "That does it. She's out of here. If you could find out that easily, anyone can."

"But who else would be inclined to check?"

"I can't answer that question, and that's exactly why she has to go."

Salvatore looked at his grandson in silence. "Why is she here, Adam? Does it have to do with me? Did you buy their cooperation by bringing Tori into the house?"

The muscle in Adam's jaw moved, but he said nothing.

"So that's it. And unless I miss my guess, Tori isn't any more pleased about the situation you've found yourselves in than you are."

"It wasn't her doing, if that's what you mean."

"Then I suggest you remember that when the two of you are together."

"The problems between us stem from other sources."

"Can you tell me why she's here? What does she hope to accomplish?"

"The arrest of Angelo Fortuna."

"For the murder of Brian?"

"For tax evasion. I'm supposed to lure Fortuna into a false sense of well-being, get him to try to buy us out and when he produces the cash, nail him."

"But you don't want to do that," Salvatore finished for him.

"That's right. It's too easy. I want him to pay for Brian, and I want it on the record books that he's paying for Brian."

"And where does that leave Tori?"

"Back in her office in Washington where she belongs."

Salvatore looked at him quietly. "She belongs with you."

Adam stared out at the Sound. "No. I thought so, too, at one time, but now I know better."

"May I make a suggestion?"

Adam's mouth curved slightly. "You will whether I want you to or not."

"Don't tell her I know who she is, and don't send her away. I've kind of enjoyed having the FBI leave me in peace. If she goes back empty-handed, they'll be all over me again."

Adam sat on the bench Tori had vacated earlier and sighed. "That was my purpose in agreeing to having her here in the first place."

"Then it won't hurt for a little longer. We don't want them snooping around—particularly now. It could cause problems."

"We already have problems."

"What are you talking about?"

"Rumblings have already started in some of the other families about getting their hands on your holdings. Even members of our own family are getting restless."

Salvatore's gaze was unwavering. "What aren't you telling me?"

Adam hesitated before speaking. "Ciccio DiMaera was hit late last night."

"You were supposed to meet with him."

"I did. He was shot outside the restaurant. He's in the hospital now. He's going to be all right."

"And where were you?"

"Just coming outside. If Sesto hadn't slammed me to the pavement I would have been hit, too."

Salvatore closed his eyes and slowly shook his head. "My God. Where will this madness end?" Then he opened his eyes and pierced Adam with his look. "Do you know who did it?"

"Not for sure, but it looks like it was Angelo Fortuna."

"Damn him. The man's an animal."

"An animal who knows what he's doing. One by one he's getting rid of the people around us until we stand alone."

"I made a mistake when I gave my word to Fortuna that we would take no action against him for Brian's murder."

"You gave your word," Adam said quietly, "but I didn't give mine."

Salvatore looked sadly at his grandson. "I never meant for this to fall on your shoulders."

"I know, but I can handle it. Within a year I'll have everything turned around. You'll be completely legitimate."

"Do you really think you can pull it off?" Salvatore asked.

"I wouldn't be here if I didn't."

"Do you think Fortuna knows what we're doing?"

Adam shook his head. "I don't think he even suspects. I have a meeting set up with him for tomorrow afternoon to negotiate his buy out of your Atlantic City and Las Vegas interests."

"And isn't he going to be surprised when he finds out that we're selling out hotel shares to some legitimate businessmen."

"Surprised and angry."

"This meeting," Salvatore continued as though he hadn't heard Adam's last remark, "is it in our territory or his?"

"Ours. He insisted on coming to the house because he knows we would never allow anything to happen to him here."

"Maybe he's not as dumb as I thought. Is he coming alone?"

"He'll be with one bodyguard."

"That's good." Salvatore grew thoughtful. "So, he wants to negotiate. How far are you going to let him take it?"

"As far as I have to until we can finish negotiations with the other men."

Salvatore's eyes rested on Adam. "You watch your back. He's not to be trusted. He might figure that if he gets rid of you, there'll be no one here to handle this. That's why he killed Brian." He shook his head. "It was all so pointless. You were the power, not Brian. His death accomplished nothing." He looked at Adam. "Don't let anything happen to yourself."

"I'm being very careful." Adam rose and put his hands on the back of the wheelchair. "Come on. I'll take you back to the house. It's getting cold out here."

When Tori had gotten back to the house, she'd run up to her room and looked out the window at the two men talking. It was obvious that something very serious was being discussed and she could only wonder what it was. What she should do is call her boss and have herself taken off of the assignment. But if she did that it would mean going after Salvatore again. Now that she'd met him, she wasn't sure that was the best thing. What good would it do, really?

And last but not least, she didn't want Adam facing Angelo Fortuna alone. She was worried about him. What had happened to Brian could so easily happen to Adam.

Tori focused on Adam again. She'd always believed that she would be the one to choose the man she'd eventually fall in love with. There were certain criteria he'd be expected to meet. It had all seemed so logical. It had never occurred to her that it could be taken so completely out of her hands.

Adam turned his head suddenly and looked right at her as though he'd known she was there all along. Tori didn't move. She just looked back, her heart in her eyes. But he was too far away to notice. Then he turned away from her and continued speaking with Salvatore.

With a sigh, Tori left the bedroom and went downstairs to the kitchen.

She found Mrs. Rosetti there, chopping vegetables. It was a wonderful kitchen, completely up-to-date, probably recently remodeled. And yet for all of its modern conveniences, it managed to maintain a lovely old-fashioned warmth and friendliness that embraced whoever entered. And the smell of fresh bread coming from the double ovens was just short of heaven.

Mrs. Rosetti looked up from what she was doing and smiled. "Well, hello again, dear. How was your walk?"

"Very nice, thank you. I seem to have worked up an appetite. Is there something I could get myself to eat?"

"I could make you a sandwich."

"Oh, no, thank you anyway. I was thinking more in terms of an apple or an orange."

Mrs. Rosetti looked Tori over and shook her head disapprovingly. "You don't eat enough."

"I've been a little nervous lately. Wait until I settle down. Then I'll do your cooking the justice it deserves."

"You and your husband both. A big man like that ought to eat more. The apples are in the refrigerator. And while you're over there, would you please take the bread out of the oven and set it on the cooling rack? The pot holders are in that drawer." She aimed the knife across the kitchen.

Tori found the pot holders and did as she'd been asked, deeply inhaling the smell that was like no other as she set the loaves down. Then she went to the refrigerator for her apple and brought it with her to munch as she sat on a stool near the counter and watched Mrs. Rosetti's thick fingers skillfully slicing carrots.

"How do you like your new home?"

"It's lovely." Tori leaned her elbows on the butcher block. "Have you worked here long?"

Mrs. Rosetti smiled as she thought about it. "As a matter of fact, my husband and I just celebrated our thirtieth year with the Danaro family last month. Jake, my husband,'' she explained, ''takes care of the grounds.''

''After all those years—'' Tori tread lightly, nonchalantly ''—you must know a lot about the Danaro family.''

Mrs. Rosetti shook her head and smiled. ''I could tell you stories...if I was one to gossip, which I'm not. Do you like celery?''

''Love it.''

The cook handed her a stalk and went back to chopping. ''The Danaros are an interesting family, I have to admit. Always have been. And I don't care what anybody says, and that includes the newspapers, they're good people. Every last one of them, the grandchildren included.''

''What about Adam?''

Mrs. Rosetti's knife stopped for a moment. ''Adam was different from the others. He was always the quiet one. More interested in buildings than in people, but able to get along with everyone. He's not easy to read, though. I didn't know what he was thinking when he was a child and I don't know what he's thinking now.''

Tori could relate to that.

''He left here right out of high school,'' Mrs. Rosetti continued, once again chopping her vegetables, but more slowly, pausing every now and again. ''Wouldn't take a dime from the family, but didn't turn his back on them, either.''

''I understand his parents died when he was small.''

The cook nodded. "It was hard on all of the kids, growing up without a mother for most of their lives, and then to have their father taken away from them at such a young age as well. I did the best I could to fill in, but I had my own family to raise back then." She was silent for a moment. "Sometimes I think this family is cursed. First Salvatore's son and daughter-in-law, then his wife and oldest grandson. It's tragic."

And senseless, Tori thought.

Her appetite suddenly left her and Tori dropped the apple into the wastebasket next to her. Even the celery wasn't looking that good anymore.

"I think you'll enjoy meeting the rest of the family," Mrs. Rosetti continued.

"I met Caroline yesterday."

Mrs. Rosetti nodded with a smile, her eyes on her work. "That girl is always on the go. It's exhausting just trying to keep up with her."

"Does she work?"

"Indeed she does, for an advertising firm. And then there's Joey, the baby. He's twenty-seven now and just got married a few months ago." The cook looked meaningfully at Tori. "Wait until you meet his wife."

"Why?"

"She's a Las Vegas showgirl. All legs. Hair out to here—" she indicated a space about a foot and a half away from her head "—and makeup that's applied with a spatula. But that's Joey for you. He likes flash."

"Where do they live?"

"Here and there. Mostly Las Vegas. Joey doesn't really have a job. I don't know for sure, but I think old Mr. Danaro supports him. But he's a good boy. He just hasn't decided what it is he wants to do yet." Mrs. Rosetti picked up the cutting board and scraped the vegetables into a large pot. "That should be ready in time for dinner." She looked meaningfully at Tori. "You *are* going to be here for dinner, right?"

"I'll definitely be here."

"And your husband?"

"I can't really speak for him."

The cook shook her head. "You'd better take more control, dear."

Tori got to her feet. "I think I'll wander around the house a little bit. I still haven't had a grand tour."

"Enjoy yourself. It's a beautiful place."

Tori went from room to room, looking but not really seeing. When she got to the living room, she went to the window and looked out. Adam must have brought Salvatore in already because they were no longer by the Sound.

With a sigh, she turned and walked out of the room. Hands suddenly reached out and caught her shoulders just as she crashed into a solid length of body. Tori looked up and into Adam's eyes. "I'm sorry," she gasped as she stepped back. "I wasn't paying attention to where I was walking."

"So I gathered." His hands fell to his sides. "Actually, I was looking for you."

"Why?"

"I want you to do something for me."

Tori waited.

"Sam Lange, my attorney, is meeting with some people tomorrow. I can't go, but I want you to sit in for me, not in a business sense, but a social one."

"What people?"

"Just some businessmen from Las Vegas and their wives. Legitimate businessmen," he emphasized.

"Why can't you go?"

"I accidentally scheduled two meetings for the same day."

Tori was more than a little suspicious, but didn't let Adam know that. "If it'll help, of course I will."

"Good. You and Sam should leave here around one o'clock."

"I'll be ready."

"Thank you." He looked at his watch. "Excuse me."

Tori watched as he walked to the library. Why did she get the feeling that he was up to something? Something he didn't want her involved in; something that was probably going to be occurring at the house. Why else would he be so anxious to make sure she wasn't going to be here tomorrow afternoon?

Chapter Four

Tori was walking across the compound. She was feeling incredibly happy, though she didn't really know why. Maybe it was because of the beautiful, sunny day. She spotted Adam in the distance and waved to him. He started to walk toward her. Then, out of nowhere, another man appeared behind Adam. It was Angelo Fortuna. Tori stopped walking and stared. Angelo had a gun in the hand hanging by his side. After a moment he stopped walking, too, and slowly raised the hand until the gun was pointed right at Adam. Tori watched in horror. She tried to scream. To yell a warning for Adam to look out, but no sound came out. She tried again and again. Nothing. Suddenly a shot rang out and Adam went down....

Tori sat straight up in bed, her breath coming in short gasps, a fine film of perspiration covering her face. Her heart was pounding so hard that her chest ached with it. She slowly focused on her surroundings. She was in her room, in bed. It was still dark out. She closed her eyes and exhaled shakily. It had just been a dream—a horrible, horrible dream.

Reaching across to her end table, she turned on a lamp and looked at the bed. Adam wasn't there. He hadn't come back yet. Or maybe he *had* come back but just hadn't made it to bed yet. She had to make sure he was all right.

Tori snatched her robe from the end of the bed and put it on as she ran downstairs through the dimly lit house. She saw a light coming from the living room and ran in, then stood in the doorway, breathless, her heart still pounding, and looked at Adam who was standing near the fireplace.

The moment he looked at her, Adam knew something was wrong. Forgetting about the tension between them, he crossed the room and stood in front of her. "What's wrong? Are you all right?"

Her eyes devoured him. "I'm fine now. I was worried about you."

"About me?"

"I had a nightmare."

"Do you want to talk about it?"

Tori shook her head. "No. I just want to forget it." She suddenly reached up and gently touched his face with the tips of her fingers. "Please don't let anything happen to yourself."

Adam covered her hand with his and held it there, a frown creasing his forehead. "I'm being very careful, Victoria. You really don't need to worry about me."

"I can't help it." She looked at him for a long moment, then turned away, afraid that he'd see what she was feeling.

"Why did you leave me in Paris the way you did?" Adam suddenly asked. "No call. No note. You just disappeared from the face of the earth."

Tori stopped, but it was a moment before she turned and looked at him. "Because I'd fallen in love with you and I knew that there was no way you'd ever be able to forgive me for deceiving you the way I had, or for being what I was."

The muscle in his cheek moved. "I spent a year looking for you."

Her eyes gazed into his. "I'm sorry. I really am. I thought you'd just forget about me and move on."

"Is that what you did?"

"No," she said quietly. "I never forgot, and I never moved on."

"And you never bothered to get in touch with me again."

"I couldn't see the point. There was no future for us when we were in Paris and there's no future for us now."

"You give up easily."

Tori shook her head. "I just have a good grip on reality." She looked at him a moment longer, then quietly turned away. "Good night, Adam."

Tori went back to the bedroom and stood in the dark staring through the window. She was torn between being glad things between them were out in the open and sorry she'd said anything at all.

With a sigh, she looked toward the bed. There wasn't a way in the world she was going to get back to sleep. What she needed was a nice long walk. It was a good night for it, and she always felt better after a little exercise. It only took her a moment to change into jeans and a heavy sweater. Then she made her way back downstairs and outside. The brisk air felt good as it washed over her face. She could almost feel the color returning to her cheeks.

With her hands in her pockets, she struck out across the driveway, the gravel crunching under her feet, and made her way across the wooded center of the compound toward Long Island Sound.

As she approached and saw the lights reflected in the Sound, she started feeling better. It was beautiful here, and Tori had always been deeply affected by things of beauty. She sat on the same bench she'd been on earlier in the day with Salvatore and just looked. The sky was black and cloudless. She could make out star patterns. The light of a jet blinked overhead and moved slowly and noiselessly across the sky. Tori took a deep breath and exhaled. She couldn't remember the last time she'd actually taken the trouble to look at a clear night sky like this. She was going to have to remember to do it more often.

Feeling a lot more calm than she had earlier, Tori started walking along the perimeter of the compound on the cinder sidewalk. She liked the sound of the crunch under her feet. But then she heard a noise that hadn't been made by her. She stopped and listened, but now all the noises she heard belonged. She didn't turn and look. If someone was following her, she didn't want them aware that she'd been alerted.

Tori started walking again, forcing her muscles to relax. The worst thing anyone could do if they thought there was going to be trouble was to tense up.

Then it happened. A man's arm came around her throat. Without even thinking about it, Tori jabbed him in the stomach sharply with her elbow and then grabbed his free arm in both of her hands and brought it straight down, sending the man into a somersault he never expected and into a hard landing on the ground he could do nothing to break. The wind was completely knocked out of him and he lay there helplessly gasping for breath. A gun she hadn't noticed before was on the ground beside him and she quickly bent to pick it up.

"Freeze!" a voice yelled before she got to it. "If you so much as twitch, lady, you're dead."

Tori stopped in her tracks, standing like a statue, her hand still outstretched.

"Straighten up and turn around. Slowly."

She did. A man stood there, his gun trained on her. "Who are you?"

"Victoria Danaro."

"Do you think I was born yesterday? There is no Victoria Danaro."

"There is now. I just got here yesterday. You can check if you want."

"Count on it." He waved his gun. "Start walking back to the house." As they moved forward, he paused by the still winded man and shook his head in disgust. "Get up, Vito. Have a little pride."

The man marched her back through the compound, into the house and straight through to the library. Tori looked helplessly at Adam, barely noticing the man who was with him. "I'm glad you're still up," Tori said, her relief evident in her voice.

Adam looked from Tori to the man she was with, a dark brow raised. "What's going on?"

"You wouldn't believe it if I told you, sir," the man with the gun said.

The other fellow came in at that moment, leaves in his hair and on his suit, his shirt tails hanging out.

Adam rose and walked around his desk. "What the hell happened to you?"

He looked at Tori and pointed. "*She* happened to me."

A corner of Adam's mouth lifted. "Are you telling me that this little person—" he gestured toward Tori "—did this to you?"

"She's stronger than she looks, sir."

Adam quickly suppressed a smile as he looked at Tori. "Are you all right?"

"I'm fine. Just a little embarrassed. I assumed I'd be able to walk freely around the compound."

"Now you know better. You can have all the freedom you want, but check with me or someone with security first."

"I will." She turned to the two men. "I'm sorry for the trouble I caused. It won't happen again."

"Accept our apologies, Mrs. Danaro. We didn't know." They left the room and Tori found herself looking at Adam.

He shook his head. "Only you."

"Only I what?"

"Could get into a mess like that. What were you doing walking around at—" he looked at his watch "—four o'clock in the morning?"

"I couldn't get back to sleep."

"Were you thinking about that dream again?"

"I was thinking about a lot of things. I thought a walk would help to clear my mind."

"And did it?"

"Yes, as a matter of fact, it did quite nicely—until I was attacked by those men."

"And now?"

"I'm afraid my adrenaline is working overtime."

The other man in the room cleared his throat.

"Sorry, Sam," Adam apologized as the other man rose. "I'd like you to meet my wife, Victoria. Victoria, this is Sam Lange. We talked about him earlier."

"I remember." She extended her hand. "I understand we're having lunch together tomorrow."

The attorney, who looked to be about Adam's age and was as blond as Adam was dark, shook her hand

and smiled pleasantly. "That's right. I'm looking forward to it more than ever now that I've met you."

"Down, Sam," Adam said. "She's taken and so are you."

"Sorry."

"I think that's all for tonight, Sam. Go home and get some sleep. You've had a long week."

"You can say that again." The attorney winked at Tori. "It was a pleasure meeting you, Victoria. I'll see you tomorrow."

"Good night."

When the attorney had gone, Adam put his hands on Tori's shoulders and turned her to face him. "Do you want to tell me about your dream yet?"

Her eyes looked into his. Adam could be so gentle. If he ever really fell in love with a woman, she would be someone to be envied. "It's over with and I'd just like to forget it. I feel kind of silly about it now."

"FBI agents aren't supposed to have bad dreams?"

"FBI agents aren't supposed to overreact, which is exactly what I did."

His eyes rested on her lovely face. "Well, don't feel too guilty about it. I've been having my share of bad dreams lately, too."

"What are yours about?"

"Different things."

Adam appeared to have called a truce between them. Tori was torn between being relieved and wishing he'd go back to the way he'd been earlier. Her feelings were easier to handle when she was angry with him.

"Are you tired?" he asked.

"Not really."

"Good. Come with me." He put his hands on her shoulders and turned her toward the door and in the general direction of the living room.

"Where are we going?"

"To have a drink, sit in front of a fire and talk."

When they got to the living room, they discovered that the fire had long ago burned itself out. Adam rebuilt it in just a few minutes until it flickered brightly in the room, the only light.

"What would you like?" he asked as he walked over to the bar.

"Cognac." Tori sat on the floor in front of the fireplace, her back against the couch and watched as Adam poured one for her and one for himself, then crossed the room and sat down next to her with a tired sigh.

"Are you sure you wouldn't rather just go to bed?" Tori asked as she wrapped her fingers around the snifter.

"I'm tired, but I wouldn't be able to sleep. I have too much on my mind."

"Anything you want to talk about?"

He slid down so that the back of his head rested against the couch cushion. "I'd love to but I can't."

"You mean you can't with me."

He turned his head and looked at her. "If you were me, would you trust you?"

She thought about it for a moment.

"Be honest."

A hint of a smile touched her mouth. "You're going to make me say it, aren't you? All right, if you insist. No, I wouldn't trust me at all."

"Thank you." He sipped his drink and sighed. "God, I'm tired."

"I'm not surprised. You keep terrible hours. If I were really your wife, I'd—"

"You *are* really my wife."

"You know what I mean."

"Oh, I know all right. But the fact is that you're my wife. It's all very legal and binding."

She turned her head on the couch and met his look. Their faces were only inches apart. "Words on paper, Adam, that's all we have."

He raised his hand and gently trailed his fingers down her cheek to her throat. He felt her pulse against his fingertips and raised his eyes to hers.

They sat like that for a long time, neither speaking. Tori swallowed hard. She wanted nothing more than to move those few inches closer to him. To feel his breath against her face, his mouth against hers.

"Go to bed, Victoria."

She looked at him for a moment longer, then set her glass down and rose without saying anything.

When she got upstairs, she closed the bedroom door behind her and leaned against it. She was still in love with him. Wouldn't it ever stop?

She was awake an hour later when Adam came to bed. She felt the weight of his body as he sank onto the mattress. She heard his tired sigh.

Slowly she opened her eyes and studied his profile in the darkened room. Then Adam turned onto his side. Their eyes met. Neither said anything. They just looked at each other.

When Tori awoke the next morning, Adam was already gone. Today, she thought as she dressed in jeans and a white tunic shirt that she belted low on her hips, she was going to think about her job and not about Adam as an individual. There was no sense in thinking about what might have been had they been able to get together. It wasn't going to happen—it couldn't. As she'd said to Adam, she had a good grip on reality. That grip had slipped a little lately, but no more. The simple fact was that she was in love with him, and that wasn't likely to change anytime soon. And even if she couldn't forget about her feelings, she could work around them. He could bait her all he wanted; she wasn't going to let it get to her. Everything was going to go smoothly. She looked at herself in the mirror and shook her head. Sure it was.

When she got outside, Tori raised her face to the sun. It was a bright day, and unexpectedly warm. She spotted one of the family's security men standing not far from the house and walked over to him. "Hi. I was wondering if it would be all right for me to go for a walk this morning."

"Sure. Just make sure you stay in the compound, Mrs. Danaro."

"Thank you." She started off on a different route than she'd taken the night before, following the winding gravel road through the compound rather than going straight to the Sound.

She had to hand it to Salvatore. He'd known what he was doing when he built this compound thirty years earlier. It was almost as though he'd taken forty acres of forest, put a long drive through it, and built houses among the trees, all without really disturbing the natural beauty. Walking through here was a little like taking a quiet walk in the woods. There was no sound of traffic. The only noise she heard was the rustling of birds and the wind in trees.

As Tori rounded a corner, she saw a shirtless man jogging toward her. Her heart immediately went into her throat, but she forced it back down. She knew who it was before she could see his face, and frankly, when Adam got closer, it wasn't his face she was looking at. He stopped when he got to where she was, his dog beside him. He'd apparently run a long way, judging from the sweat glistening from his torso. Even his hair was wet. But he was only a little out of breath. "You're up early this morning."

"I got as much sleep as I needed," she told him, making a massive effort to keep her eyes above his neck. Why did he have to be so attractive? "Do you run every morning?"

"Every morning that I can. You should try it."

Tori shook her head. "Walking, maybe. Running, never."

"What kind of exercise do you like, then?"

Tori thought for a moment. "I tolerate tennis."

"But you prefer to watch."

"Exactly."

"Your heart needs exercise."

A smile touched Tori's mouth as their eyes met. "I prefer to keep my heart sedentary. It's safer."

"And do you always do the safe thing, Victoria?"

"Whenever possible."

His eyes met and held hers. "And what about when it's not?"

"Then I become very careful."

A corner of his mouth lifted. "Good luck." Adam started to run off, but Tori stopped him.

"Adam, have you done anything about meeting with Angelo Fortuna?"

He turned and faced her. "I told you not to concern yourself with him."

"And I told you that that's why I'm here. If you're working with him, I want to know what you're doing."

"I'll tell you what I think you need to know."

She couldn't believe what she was hearing. "Adam, I—"

Adam moved so close to her that Tori had to look up at him. "Listen, Victoria, you may think you know how to take care of yourself in dangerous situations, but you don't know Angelo Fortuna. He's not a man to be taken lightly."

"I never for a moment thought he was."

"I don't want you to get personally involved with him. If it was up to me, I wouldn't even let him know you exist."

"But . . ."

"No 'buts.' He's the kind of man who goes after the families of his enemies. And in case you've forgotten—" his eyes roamed over her face "—you're now my family. You're my wife."

"I haven't forgotten."

"I want you to stay out of his way. I'll handle what has to be handled."

"Adam, I'm not some woman you have to take care of."

"That's right. You're not some woman." Brown eyes looked into blue. "You're my woman, for now, at least. And you're my responsibility."

Tori just looked at him, too surprised to speak.

"I know what this man is capable of, Victoria. More so than you with your wiretaps and files could ever know. I want you to stay away from him."

Tori shook her head. "Oh, no, Adam Danaro. You don't tell me what to do. I've tried to be nice to you ever since I got here. I've been riddled with guilt over our trip to Paris, and I've had feelings of my own to deal with. But this is work, not personal. Now I want to know what's going on here. You made an agreement."

"I made an agreement to allow you to pose as my wife and to gather information about Angelo Fortuna."

"Exactly."

"And I intend to do just that. But from a distance. And if that isn't satisfactory to you, you can call your boss and then the two of you can take your files on my grandfather to the Attorney General."

Suddenly Tori knew what was going on. "You don't want him arrested on income tax evasion charges, do you? You want him arrested for murder."

Adam said nothing.

"But you know as well as I do that there's no direct evidence linking him with Brian's death."

"Which is not to say that it doesn't exist. Only that it hasn't yet been found." He put his hand under Tori's chin and raised her eyes to his. "You conjecture all you want, Victoria, but stay away from Angelo Fortuna." And with that, he walked away from her and toward the house.

Tori stared after him. He couldn't do this alone. Why couldn't he see that he needed help—even if it was hers?

Forgetting about her walk, Tori headed back to the house. Well, he was going to get her help whether he wanted it or not. It was just going to take a little more work than the income tax evasion charges.

She shook her head as she walked. Who was she kidding? A little more work? She could be here for the rest of her natural life.

Chapter Five

When Tori got back to the house, the first thing she did was run upstairs to get her car keys. She needed to talk to Charlie but she didn't want to call from the house in case someone else was listening in. She found the keys on her dresser, grabbed them and raced out of the room and outside to her car. When she got to the gate, the same man who'd been there when she'd arrived a few days earlier came out of the guardhouse and approached her car. "Hello, Mrs. Danaro. What can I do for you today?"

"I'd like you to open the gate. I have some errands to run."

"I'm afraid I can't do that."

"What are you talking about?"

"I have instructions from Mr. Danaro that you aren't to leave the compound without his permission."

Tori's mouth parted in surprise. "What?"

"I'm sorry, ma'am."

"It's not your fault, but there must be some mistake. I'll talk to Adam."

She drove back to the house and went inside. She found Adam in the library talking with Sam Lange. "Excuse the interruption," she said as she entered without even knocking, "but I'd like to know why the guard at the gate has been instructed not to let me out of here."

Adam leaned back in his chair, his eyes on her. "Because that's the way I want it."

"Well, that certainly explains everything."

"Where exactly is it that you want to go?"

She looked at the attorney and was reluctant to answer.

"That's all right." Adam correctly read her look. "You can talk in front of Sam."

She looked at the attorney again, then at Adam. "I want to make a phone call."

"You can make it from the house."

"I prefer not to. Now please tell the guard to let me out of here."

Adam thought about it for a moment longer. "All right. I'll call him."

"Now?"

"Now."

"Thank you." Tori turned and left the room.

Adam looked at Sesto who was standing just inside the library door, and inclined his head. Sesto wordlessly left the library and followed Tori outside.

This time when Tori got to the gate, it opened. She drove down the road for about a mile until she came to a pay phone. As she parked in front of it, she noticed a car stopping behind her about half a block away. "Honestly, Adam," she said softly in the empty car, "what do you think I'm going to do? Make a run for it?"

Tori used her credit card to call Washington, then stood in the phone booth with the receiver against her ear and watched the other car. It looked like Sesto was behind the wheel. As soon as she heard Charlie's voice, she pulled a pen and a slip of paper from her purse and turned her back on Sesto. "Charlie, this is Tori. I need some information."

"Sure."

"I want to know if Angelo Fortuna is seeing or living with anyone."

"Hold on a minute. I'll check."

Tori drummed her fingers on the cold metal of the small ledge beneath the phone and waited. Charlie came back on about three minutes later. "He's living with a Georgette Lowell."

"Thanks."

"Why do you need to know that?"

"I'm not sure yet."

"Is everything all right, Tori? You sound a little strange."

"Everything is fine."

"Are you making any progress on Angelo Fortuna?"

"I've only been here two days, Charlie. Give me a chance."

"Right. Sorry. It's just that I got to thinking about what you said the other night."

"What was that?"

"About Adam Danaro simply buying time for his grandfather and then leaving us in the cold."

"He won't do that. We'll come out of this with something."

"How can you be so sure?"

"Because getting Angelo Fortuna behind bars is a matter of honor with him." She didn't mention that he wanted to do it on a murder charge rather than tax evasion.

"Well, you know the guy better than I do. Be careful, will you?"

"Don't worry about me. Adam has me so closely watched that I'd be amazed if a mosquito could get to me."

"Good. Anything else?"

"Not right now."

"Okay. Keep in touch."

When Tori hung up, she pocketed the slip of paper and climbed back into her car. Traffic was light, so she made a U-turn. Stopping next to Sesto's car, she rolled down her window. "I'm going straight back to the house now."

The bodyguard had the grace to smile a little. "Yes, ma'am."

By the time she returned to the compound, it was getting a little late. She went upstairs to dress for lunch. After a lot of debate in front of her closet, Tori decided on a marine-blue suit. The long jacket was large on top and then grew narrow toward her hips. The slim-fitting skirt was also marine blue, as were her pumps.

When she got downstairs about fifteen minutes later, the attorney was already waiting for her. His eyes appreciatively covered her from head to toe. "Nice."

"Thank you."

He held out his arm. "We'd better get going. I don't want to keep these people waiting."

"Who exactly are they?"

"Just some businessmen and their wives."

"Adam said they were legitimate."

"They are."

"Then why are you meeting with them?"

"Ouch!" he said as he opened the car door for her. "You don't pull your punches, do you?"

She waited until he settled himself into the driver's side before saying anything else. "Why do you work for the Danaros? You're presumably a good attorney, or they wouldn't have hired you."

"Meaning I could work anywhere?"

"Exactly."

"Well, I intend to go elsewhere in the not-too-distant future. But for now I'm helping out Adam."

"Helping him to do what?"

Sam looked at her from the corner of his eye as he put the car into gear and headed away from the compound. "I didn't say I was helping him with anything specific. I simply said I was helping him. He's a friend."

"Aren't you worried about ruining your reputation?"

He shook his head. "I don't have any political aspirations, which is the only thing I'd really have to concern myself with. Otherwise, the Danaros only hire the best and everyone knows it. If anything, my reputation has been enhanced."

The French restaurant was only about a fifteen-minute drive from the house. Tori noticed that once again a bodyguard was in tow, traveling about half a block behind them the entire way.

When they walked into the restaurant, Tori wasn't at all surprised to find that the people Sam had said they were meeting weren't there yet. She didn't expect that they'd show up at all. This whole thing was nothing more than a ruse to get her out of the house.

Sam made a good show of it, she had to give him credit. He sat there for nearly twenty minutes, looking at his watch. "Well," he finally said, "it looks like they aren't going to make it. You'd think they'd at least call."

"That would have been the polite thing," she agreed.

"What do you think you're going to have?" he asked as he studied his own menu.

Tori told him, then put her napkin onto the table and rose. "Would you mind ordering for me? I'm going to the ladies' room.

"No problem."

"Thank you. I'll just be a moment."

Tori walked to the front of the restaurant and found the maître d'. "Excuse me, but is there a rear exit?"

He gave her a strange look, but shrugged. It wouldn't be the first time a woman had ditched her date in such a manner. "Of course. Straight back and through the kitchen."

She handed him ten dollars. "Thank you."

"My pleasure."

Tori walked casually through the kitchen, smiling at the employees who stopped working to watch her. The door opened onto an alley. If she turned right, she knew she'd run straight into the bodyguard, so she turned left and followed the alley until it emptied onto a main street. After that it only took her a moment to hail a taxi which drove her straight back to the compound. The man in the guardhouse opened the door at her knock and looked at her in surprise. "Mrs. Danaro?"

"Hi." She walked past him and out the other door which opened into the compound and headed up the drive on foot, aware that behind her the guard was calling Adam to let him know she was back.

Adam opened the front door just as she was climbing the steps. "What are you doing here? You're supposed to be at lunch."

"I know, but the guests never showed up so I thought I'd come back here."

"Where's Sam?"

"Still at the restaurant I imagine."

"You just left him there?"

"That's right."

Adam swore softly.

Tori was unaffected. "Life around here would be a lot simpler if you'd only tell me what's going on. I'll find out eventually anyway. You should know that."

The gates swung open again at that moment and a car entered the compound. Adam suddenly stiffened. "Go inside."

"What?" she asked in surprise.

"I want you to go inside and upstairs right now. Don't ask questions." He put his hands on her shoulders and turned her around, then gave her a gentle push toward to the door. "Go on."

This was too much. "Stop treating me like a child."

Adam's eyes bored into hers. "If you don't go upstairs right now under your own steam," he said evenly, "I'll throw you over my shoulder and carry you. Understand?"

He'd do it, too. Rather than go through that ignominy, she went upstairs, but stopped in the upstairs hallway long enough to look out the window to see who the visitor was. A big man, nearly as large as Sesto, stepped out of the black car first and opened the rear door. Another man stepped out and Tori recognized him immediately from his file picture—he was Angelo Fortuna.

As she watched, Angelo extended his hand. Adam hesitated only a moment before accepting the gesture. Then the two men, followed by Angelo's bodyguard, entered the house. She heard the door to the library close, and sighed. What she wouldn't give to be a bug on the wall of that room.

Another car pulled up at that moment and Sam got out. He looked furious as he stormed into the house.

Tori turned with a half smile and walked down the hall to Salvatore's room and knocked.

"Come in."

His voice was weaker than it had been. Tori opened the door and looked in with a smile. He was lying in bed looking out the window. "Hello. Would you like some company?"

"I thought you went out to lunch."

"I'm back."

Salvatore smiled and shook his head. "I told Adam it wouldn't work."

"He should listen to you more often."

His smile faded. "You know why he did it, don't you?"

"I have a fairly good idea."

"He doesn't want you to cross Angelo Fortuna's path."

"Then all he had to do was ask me nicely to stay out of the way. There's no need for elaborate plots."

"And what would you have done if he had?"

A smile touched her mouth. "I'm not sure."

"Neither was he."

"Point taken."

Tori came the rest of the way into the room and sat on the chair next to the bed. "That's enough about me. How are you feeling today?"

He sighed and closed his eyes. "Tired. Very tired."

Tori put her hand on top of his and gave it a soft squeeze. He didn't look at all well. "Would you like me to read to you, or just leave you alone?"

"Reading would be nice."

She picked up the book from the bedside table and opened it to the marked page. In her soft, low voice, she began to read, but her thoughts were downstairs with Adam.

"Tori?"

Salvatore's voice interrupted the flow of her words. "Would you please go to the kitchen and get me some orange juice?"

"Certainly." She set the book on the table, noticing in surprise that more than an hour had passed since she'd come upstairs. "I'll be right back."

When she got to the bottom of the stairs, she found Sesto near the library door, but this time, rather than sitting, he was standing, legs apart, arms folded across his chest. Angelo Fortuna's bodyguard stood on the other side of the door in a similar stance, watching her with unfriendly eyes. Tori took a deep breath and forced what she hoped was a natural smile. Whenever she saw people like these hulking bodyguards, she couldn't help but think about what they'd do to her if they found out who she was. This was a dangerous game she was playing, and every once in a while it hit home. She was very much in enemy territory.

Just as she started to walk past them, the library door opened and Angelo Fortuna stood silhouetted in the sunlight streaming through the library windows. "I want you to settle on a firm price within the week,

Danaro." As he turned to leave, his eyes alighted on Tori and he stopped, a suggestive smile playing at the corners of his mouth. "Well, hello there."

This man was obviously a victim of too much television. He had on a rich blue sport coat with the sleeves pushed up, showing off a fancy, clunky watch that had no purpose other than to tell people that he could afford to spend thousands of dollars on something that told time. He also wore a bright yellow T-shirt and baggy blue pants. His cheeks sported a three day growth of beard in an apparent attempt to make his strange baby face appear more rugged. If she hadn't known just how dangerous he was, she would have been tempted to laugh. "Hello," she said politely. "Excuse me."

As she started to walk past him, Angelo's hand shot out and caught her arm. "I don't think I will." His eyes moved very slowly and suggestively down her slender body, sending a shiver of distaste coursing through her. "No, I don't think I'll excuse you at all. Who are you?"

Adam came out of his office at that moment. The look he gave Tori was more eloquent than words. "She's my wife."

Angelo's fingers tightened painfully on her arm for a moment before his hand fell to his side. "That's too bad."

Tori could tell from the way Angelo looked at her that he was attracted. There had to be some way she could use that against him. But how? Particularly since Adam would see to it that they never met again.

"What are you doing down here?" Adam asked.

"I was getting your grandfather a glass of orange juice."

"Then do it."

"Of course. I'm sorry for interrupting." When she got to the swinging kitchen door, she turned and looked behind her. Angelo, Adam and the two bodyguards were just disappearing around the corner. Adam, as though sensing her eyes on him, turned his head and looked straight at her. Tori couldn't have moved if she'd wanted to, such was the intensity of his gaze. Then Adam wordlessly turned the corner and walked out of sight.

Tori went through the swinging kitchen door and sat down in the nearest chair, her hand over her racing heart. How could he do that to her with just a look?

She stayed like that for several minutes, then realized that the reason she'd come downstairs in the first place was to get Salvatore some juice. Going to the refrigerator, she poured a tumbler full and went back to the hall. As she walked past the library, the doors were open and she looked in. No one was there. She looked down the hall and listened for any approaching footsteps. There were none.

Setting the glass on a hall table, she quietly walked into the library, closing the doors softly behind her and headed for the desk. It was immaculate. There wasn't so much as a scrap of paper lying on it. Nothing to tell her what Adam and Angelo had been discussing.

Not one to give up easily, she opened one drawer
after another, having absolutely no idea of what she
was looking for, but knowing she'd recognize it when
she found it. Something was very definitely going on.
Something to which Adam was central—and she
wanted to find out what it was. As she carefully went
through the bottom drawer, Tori stopped, her heart
suddenly pounding at the sound of voices in the hall.
One of them belonged to Adam and the other sounded
like Sam Lange's. She quietly closed the drawer and
looked around the room for a way out. Nothing. Her
heart pounded even harder at the realization that she
was trapped. Suddenly her eyes alighted on a Chinese
screen at the far end of the room. Tori sprinted toward it, managing to get behind it just as the door
opened.

With her hand over her heart, she closed her eyes
and stood there desperately trying to control her
breathlessness and slowly but surely succeeding. When
this case was finished, she was definitely going to have
to look for another line of work.

"I don't know what Angelo's trying to prove,"
Adam said as he walked into the library, "but he's
obviously up to something. I don't trust him."

Tori moved her head so that she could see through
the slivered opening between screen sections. Adam
was behind his desk, leaning back in his chair, his fingers steepled under his chin. Sam sat across from him,
his briefcase on his lap, open. "You know as well as I
do that he wants you out of here. He thinks your
grandfather should have turned to him to run things."

"Grandfather's too smart for that. Angelo has a lot higher opinion of his own intellectual prowess than anyone who knows him does."

"Do you think he knows what you're doing?"

Adam shook his head. "I don't see how he could. No one does besides you, Grandfather and me. The others I've approached have no connection with either Angelo or anyone Angelo might have influence with."

Approached about what? Tori wondered. Her nose tickled a little bit and she wriggled it.

"I have some things that need your signature," the attorney told Adam as he pulled some papers out of his briefcase and put them on the desk.

What things? Tori wondered, wriggling her nose again.

"It's going to take us at least a year to wind up all of these matters."

All of what matters? Tori quietly raised her hand to her nose and rubbed it.

"A year," Adam sighed as he picked up a pen. "That's a long time."

Tori, with indescribable horror, felt a sneeze coming on. She took a deep breath and pinched her nose, waiting for the urge to pass, which it did a few seconds later. With a relieved smile, she let go of her nose and exhaled. "Hiccup!" Tori, her eyes wide, jammed her hand against her mouth.

"What was that?" the attorney asked.

"What was what?"

"Didn't you hear a noise?"

Adam listened for a moment, then shook his head. "Must have been outside."

Tori rolled her eyes heavenward and mouthed thank you.

Adam looked at his watch and got to his feet. "I want you to try to finish up negotiations with those buyers for the Las Vegas property sometime in the next few weeks."

"All right." Sam gathered the papers Adam had signed and put them into his briefcase.

As Tori watched through the narrow crack in the screen, Adam walked the attorney out of the library. She quietly came out from behind the screen and breathed again for the first time since she'd hiccuped. It was now or never. She had to get out of here before he came back. Peering around the door and seeing no one, she stepped into the hallway and closed the library door behind her, then straightened her shoulders and headed down the hall. Suddenly she stopped. The orange juice. She'd forgotten all about it. Retracing her steps, she picked it up from the hall table and turned around only to crash right into Adam's chest.

His strong hands caught her shoulders to keep her from falling backward. How she managed not to spill the juice, she'd never know.

"I'm sorry," she apologized, stepping away from him. "I didn't know you were there."

"Obviously. You'd be amazed at what a difference watching where you walk makes."

Tori smiled, but it was tinged with guilt. "I'll try to remember that."

Adam walked past her, but stopped after a few feet and looked back. "Oh, by the way, you might try a glass of water for those hiccups of yours."

"Oh, I will, thank—" Tori stared after him as he disappeared into the library and wished the floor would slowly open up and swallow her whole.

When she finally got the juice upstairs and handed to Salvatore, he raised it to his mouth, eyeing her over the rim of the glass. "The kitchen must be farther away than I remember," he remarked as he handed her back the glass.

"I'm sorry I took so long," she apologized as she set the glass on the bedside table. "I got side-tracked." She picked up the book ready to read to him again, when there was a knock on the door and Adam walked in.

"I need to speak with you, Grandfather."

Tori put the book back and rose. "I'll excuse myself."

Adam held the door open for her. "You I'll speak with later," he informed her.

Tori's heart sank as she went to her room and paced back and forth. She hated scenes, and she had a feeling there was about to be a big one.

Maybe if she just got out of here for a while he'd have time to cool off. There'd still be a scene later, but maybe not such a major one. Grabbing her keys from the dresser, she headed out of the bedroom only to find Adam already in the hall.

He looked at the keys in her hand. "Where are you going?"

"Just out for a drive."

"No, you're not," he disagreed calmly. "You're going to meet me in my office in ten minutes."

"Your office?"

"That's right. We're going to get a few things straight between us."

"Look, I'm sorry about running into Angelo like that earlier. It was an accident. I honestly was getting your grandfather some juice. It never occurred to me that Angelo would be coming out of your office just at that moment."

"A lot of things don't seem to occur to you. But I'll tell you about those later."

"In ten minutes?"

"That's right." And with that he walked away from her and down the stairs.

Chapter Six

When Tori got to the library ten minutes later, she stood outside the door and took a deep breath before knocking.

"Come in, Victoria."

She walked in and closed the door behind her. "You wanted to see me?"

"Sit down."

She hesitated.

"Of course you can stand if you like. I just thought you might be more comfortable."

Tori sat down, her hands folded in her lap, and waited for the explosion.

Adam half sat, half leaned against the edge of his desk and looked down at her. "You're a difficult woman to control."

"I know," she said quietly.

"And ordinarily I'd like that quality, but right now it's life and death and I can't have someone around me who's going to be unpredictable."

"I understand."

"No, Victoria, you don't. That's the whole problem. And it's my fault. You're here to do a job and I'm not letting you do it. Therefore, you feel you have to work around me. I'd do the same thing if the situation were reversed."

She didn't trust his change in attitude. "What exactly are you saying?"

He walked around his desk and sat down, his eyes on hers. "I want to get things out in the open."

Tori couldn't help but wonder if this was another ploy, like having Sam take her out to lunch.

He knew what she was thinking. "Don't look at me like that, Victoria. I'm not trying to trick you. At the moment we're working at cross purposes, and one of these days we're going to collide unless we do something about it."

"I'm willing."

"Good. Oh, by the way," he said almost as an afterthought, "how are your hiccups?"

Tori couldn't help the embarrassed smile that tugged at her mouth. "All gone now, thank you." She looked at him curiously. "If you knew I was in here, why didn't you say something at the time?"

"Because I didn't want Sam to know. What were you doing, anyway?"

"After your meeting with Angelo, I knew you wouldn't tell me what had happened, so I decided to look around myself and see if you'd put something in writing that would tell me what was going on. Then I heard you coming back and I didn't have time to get out."

"So you hid behind the screen."

"Exactly."

"I thought as much. That's why I asked you to come here and talk to me. I'd prefer getting Angelo myself, but since you're here and you're no doubt going to be interfering anyway, you might as well be useful."

"Charmingly put."

"Truthfully put."

"What exactly do you envision my role to be around here?"

"Pretty much background," he replied.

"Naturally," she said dryly.

"It's necessary. In our family and in others like ours, the women simply aren't involved in business. If you're suddenly sitting in on meetings and taking notes, someone's bound to get suspicious."

"I know," she agreed quietly.

"I'll do what we agreed to in Parker's office, which means I'll provide you with pertinent information which you can pass along to him. But other than that, you're here strictly for decoration."

"How chauvinistic of you."

"That's right," he said, not visibly moved.

"Is that the way you are in real life?"

"What? Chauvinistic?"

She nodded.

"In real life. An interesting way of putting it." He thought for a moment. "I try not to be, but I suppose sometimes I am." His eyes met hers. "Particularly when I see trouble coming."

"Are you equating me with trouble?"

"Yes."

She was taken aback by his directness. "Oh."

"Just 'oh'?"

"I can't think of a witty riposte at the moment."

"That's all right. It gives me something to look forward to."

A dimple appeared in Tori's cheek. "I think I like you."

"Like? I thought you fell head over heels for me in Paris."

"That was different."

"Different how?"

"That was strictly hormones."

The grooves in Adam's cheeks deepened. "Hormones?"

Tori's cheeks filled with delightful color. "I know. I can't believe I said it either."

"You're full of surprises."

"Is that good?"

"It's . . . interesting."

"When I was growing up, being interesting was considered a romantic kiss of death."

"And what about now that you're grown?"

"I'm not sure. I'll let you know."

"Good. I'll have two things to look forward to."

Tori studied him for a moment. "You're not going to tell me what's really going on around here, are you?"

"That's right. It doesn't concern you."

Adam's eyes traveled slowly over her. She looked the same as she had in Paris, with her mane of hair and luminous eyes and their delicious twinkle. It was strange to think of a woman as being mischievous, but that's how she struck him. "You seem to have gotten your sense of adventure back."

"What do you mean?"

"When we were on the plane, and later in Paris, one of the things that drew me to you—aside from hormones, of course," he added dryly, "was how alive you were. You ignited everyone around you. I've been to Paris dozens of times, but I never loved it as much as I did when I saw it through your eyes. Then when I saw you again in Washington, you seemed different."

"I wasn't expecting to see you. When I walked into Charlie's office and saw you standing there, it was as though someone had knocked the wind out of me. It took me a while to recover."

"And now?"

Tori looked down at her hands. "Well, I'm adjusting. It's not very productive to walk around riddled with guilt and doubts about something in the past that can't be changed, and I'm not going to do it any longer."

Adam leaned back in his chair, his eyes on her. "So, the old Victoria is back, in all of her complexity."

"That's right." She looked at her watch. "If we're finished, I have to make a phone call."

"We're finished."

She got up to leave, but Adam's voice stopped her.

"Don't forget what I said."

She turned with a smile. "I know. Victoria, thy name is trouble. Knock it off."

"That's a good job of paraphrasing."

"Thank you."

"Now do you *understand* what you just paraphrased?"

"Of course." She started to leave, but stopped again. "Of course, our definitions of what 'trouble' means could be worlds apart. But why quibble? I've got the general idea. See you later."

When Tori walked into the hallway, she saw Salvatore's nurse disappearing into the kitchen.

Without hesitating, Tori went quickly upstairs and took from her purse a piece of notepaper she'd used to jot down Georgette Lowell's telephone number. Using the phone on the desk in a corner of the bedroom, Tori cradled the receiver between her ear and shoulder while she pressed out the number. It rang several times before a delightful, soft female voice answered.

"I'd like to speak with Georgette Lowell."

"This is she."

"Hello, Georgette. My name is Victoria Danaro. I recently married Adam Danaro."

"Oh, yes, I heard about that. Congratulations."

"Thank you. Am I disturbing you at all?"

"Oh, no. As a matter of fact I was hoping for a little diversion. It's been a long, boring day."

"I know what you mean. I'm from out of state and don't know anyone in Connecticut at all. Actually that's why I was calling. I thought maybe the two of us could get together over lunch one day this week."

"I'd love it! But why wait? Are you free this evening?"

Tori would have loved to have been able to say "yes," but she didn't dare. "Not for dinner."

"Oh, that's too bad." There was a pause. "How about meeting me for cocktails in an hour?"

"That would be fine. Where?"

"Do you know where Jenaro's is?"

"I don't know where anything is, but I can find it."

"Do you have a pen?"

"Just a minute." Tori rifled through her purse and pulled out pen and paper. "Go ahead."

"I know where Adam's house is, so I'll give you directions from there."

"All right."

"Turn right as you come through the gate. At the first—no, wait a minute—the second stoplight, turn right. Go for another mile or so until you get to Chestnut Street, then turn left."

"Onto Chestnut?"

"Uh-huh. Jenaro's is on Chestnut, about ten blocks from where you turn, on the right-hand side of the road."

"I've got it. Thank you."

"See you in a little while."

Tori hung up and smiled, inordinately pleased with herself. She'd learned not long after becoming an agent that the best way to learn about a man is through the woman he's closest to. She was hoping to get a real education about Angelo Fortuna tonight.

She ran back downstairs and knocked on the library door.

"Come in."

She found Adam in there talking to Sam. The attorney looked at her with a wry expression. "You missed a good lunch."

"I'm sorry. I really hated doing that to you."

"It's all right. No hard feelings. Just don't do it again, all right?"

Tori smiled and looked at Adam. "Would you please tell the fellow at the front gate that I'll be leaving in a few minutes?"

Adam looked at his watch. "It's four o'clock. Where are you going?"

"I have a few errands to run."

"What kind of errands?"

"I need to buy some things."

"I assume that. What things?"

Tori sighed. "Am I going to have to go through this every time I want to leave the compound? I feel like a prisoner."

Adam was unmoved. "What things do you need to buy, Victoria?"

"Female things," she said in exasperation. "Would you like me to be more specific?"

A corner of his mouth lifted. "You would be, too, wouldn't you?"

"Whatever it takes."

He looked at her for a moment and shook his head, but he was obviously amused. "I'll have Sesto take you."

"No!"

Adam lifted an expressive brow.

"I mean, I'd rather go in my own car. Besides, I need to buy gas. I'm really low."

"I can have someone take care of that for you."

Tori was ready to pull her hair out. "I like doing things for myself."

Adam was growing increasingly suspicious. "All right. I'll call the front gate."

"Thank you."

As soon as she left the library, Adam picked up the phone. "Sesto, my wife is going to be leaving here in a few minutes. I want you to follow her and make sure she stays out of trouble."

After Adam had hung up, Sam asked, "Don't you think you're keeping the reins just a little tight on her? After all, she *is* your wife."

"If you knew her as well as I know her, you'd be worried too," Adam said with a shake of his head. "The woman keeps me on my toes."

"I like her."

"Wait until you've known her a little longer. I promise you she'll evoke considerably stronger emotions than 'like.'"

Tori ran back upstairs and looked at herself in the mirror. She decided to keep on the marine-blue suit she'd worn to lunch. Grabbing the directions to the restaurant from the telephone desk and whipping her purse over her shoulder, she took off. When she got outside, Sesto was parked immediately behind her car, waiting.

Tori smiled at him while swearing lightly at Adam under her breath. Climbing into her car, she headed away from the compound in the direction of the restaurant. True to her word, she stopped at a drugstore to make some purchases, then at a gas station. Sesto patiently waited in his car for her at each stop.

Tori had thought of at least one sure way of getting away from Sesto. It involved going into a store through one door, coming out through another and taking a taxi to the restaurant. But as fate would have it, she didn't need to do anything so drastic. As she approached a gateless railroad crossing, the lights started flashing and bells ringing. Tori stopped and looked for the train. She saw it in the distance. It was a long one.

Her eyes went to her rearview mirror. Sesto was there, right behind her. Tori licked her lips and took a deep breath. This was her chance. She watched and waited. Her hands were gripping the steering wheel. As the train approached, Tori gritted her teeth and gunned her car across the tracks, making it to the other side just as the monster roared by.

Tori made it to the restaurant without stopping, and shook like a leaf all the way. When she finally parked her car in the lot, she turned off the engine and just sat there with her hand over her pounding heart. Never again. Next time she'd use the second door routine.

Jenaro's was, as she might have expected from the name, an Italian restaurant, but a little upscale from the friendly family restaurants she knew of. When she walked in, there was no one in the restaurant part because it was so early, but the bar was already humming with activity.

A man walked over to her with a friendly smile. "How may I help you?"

"I'm meeting someone here by the name of Georgette Lowell."

"Miss Lowell is waiting." He led her across the bar to a comfortable booth.

Tori found herself looking at a lovely, petite, blond, blond, blond, woman. "Georgette?"

The woman looked up and smiled. "Victoria? Please, have a seat."

Tori slid across from her into the booth.

"Can I get you something from the bar?" asked the man she'd followed to the table.

Ordinarily she would have had mineral water, but after the train, Tori needed something a little stronger. "Dry sherry on ice, please." Then she looked at Georgette. "I hope I didn't keep you waiting long."

"Just got here. Did you find the place all right?"

"Your directions were perfect."

"That has to be a first for me."

As the two women looked each other over, Tori knew instinctively that she was going to like Georgette Lowell.

"So you're the one who landed Adam. I've been wondering about you ever since I heard the news."

"Is he supposed to be a major catch?"

"Let's just say that I can name several who would trade places with you in an instant."

"Do you know my husband well?"

"No. I've seen him at a few dinners, but he's usually alone. He's kind of aloof from other people."

"I didn't know that."

"Of course you wouldn't. If he thought enough of you to marry you, he wouldn't be aloof with you."

Tori smiled. "I think I can safely say that aloofness is not one of the reactions I inspire in my husband." In fact, she was quite sure that losing Sesto the way she had was going to elevate Adam to a new emotional high.

"I understand you met Angelo this afternoon."

"That's right. As a matter of fact, that's what made me think of calling you. Since I'm going to be living in Connecticut now, I'd like to start meeting some people."

"And of course you and I are in somewhat special circumstances."

Tori nodded. "Exactly."

"We have to be so careful about new acquaintances."

"That's true. Does Angelo mind that you're meeting me here tonight?"

"He wasn't home when I left, so I didn't have a chance to tell him, but I'm sure not. I get so bored sometimes just sitting around."

"Don't you work?"

She shook her head and sipped her drink. "I used to be a secretary, but when I moved in with Angelo four years ago, I had to quit."

"Had to?"

"He wanted me in the house."

"Oh."

"What about you?"

"I do research for a history professor." That was the truth. Not the whole truth, but close enough.

"That sounds interesting."

"It can be. But it can also be a little dry at times."

Georgette nodded.

The waiter came with Tori's sherry. She raised her glass to Georgette. "To new acquaintances."

Georgette raised hers as well.

"So tell me," Tori said as she set her glass on the table, "how did you and Angelo meet?"

And it began. Tori sat through the first meeting and on through the very short courtship. Georgette left no detail unspoken, no gift unmentioned, no emotion unfelt. But it was strangely intriguing. She learned a lot about Angelo Fortuna. When Tori next glanced at her watch, she saw to her horror that two hours had passed. Adam would probably be frantic by now, and that certainly hadn't been her intention.

"Oh, Georgette," Tori interrupted, "I'm sorry, but I have to leave. I should have gone a while ago, but I was so engrossed...."

"Can't you stay just a little longer? It's been so long since I had anyone to talk to."

"I wish I could. Maybe we could meet again?"

"I'd like that."

Tori reached into her purse for some money, but a hand came down on her shoulder. "Please, no. Georgette and I won't hear of your paying for your drinks."

She looked up and into the cool eyes of Angelo Fortuna.

"Angelo!" Georgette beamed. "How did you know where to find me?"

"I have my ways." He sat next to Georgette, his eyes still on Tori. "How did you two happen to meet?"

"I called her," Tori said.

"I see." The way he said it sounded as though he saw all too well. It made Tori nervous. "Well, now that the three of us are here, maybe we can all have dinner."

"I can't, really," Tori apologized. "As a matter of fact, I was just leaving."

"Don't be silly. Call your husband and tell him you'll be a little late. Better yet, invite him to join us."

"Oh, I don't think so, but thank you anyway. We have other plans."

Angelo's eyes went to a point in the distance over her head. "You spoke too soon. Here he is now."

Tori turned and saw Adam walking toward her. Though it was impossible to gauge how he was feeling by his expression, Tori knew instinctively that he was furious and she cringed inwardly.

When he got to the table, Adam inclined his head toward the other man. "Angelo. Hello, Georgette." His eyes went to Tori. "You're late. I was worried."

"I'm sorry. I was just getting ready to come home."

"But now that you're here," Angelo said to Adam, "that won't be necessary. Why don't the two of you join us for dinner?"

Before Adam could say anything, Tori's ears picked up the strains of a song she'd never heard before. "Oh," she said quickly, "that's our song." She got up and took Adam's hand in hers as she smiled at the other couple. "Excuse us for a moment."

"Tori—"

She tugged on his reluctant hand. "Come on."

They moved to the middle of the empty floor. Tori stood in front of Adam and put her hand on his shoulder.

"I don't think they have dancing here," he told her.

"Then we'll start a new fad."

He put his hand at her waist and took her other hand in his.

"How did you find out where I was?" she asked.

"Sesto finally found your car after driving around for nearly two hours."

"Oh."

"Oh? Oh?"

"You're angry with me, aren't you?"

"I don't think anger quite covers what I'm feeling toward you at the moment. What the hell do you think you're doing?"

She smiled over his shoulder at Angelo and Georgette. "I wanted to get to know more about Angelo."

"I told you I didn't want you anywhere near the man."

"He wasn't supposed to be here. In fact, he arrived just before you did."

"So you've spent the past two hours talking to Georgette?"

"That's right?"

"Why?"

"So I could learn more about Angelo."

Adam shook his head. "You're incorrigible. What am I going to do with you?"

"You could let me have a little slack so I don't have to play these ridiculous games."

"If I cut you any more slack you're going to hang yourself, and me along with you."

"You may not think talking to Georgette is important, but I'm here to tell you that it's often the people you'd least expect who have the most information. You can't live with a man for as long as she has and not know what's going on. Even if it's just tidbits of conversation picked up here and there."

Adam's arm slid farther around her waist as he pulled her body tightly against his. Their faces were inches apart. "I want you to back away from Angelo right now. There will be no more discussion about it. Do you understand?"

Tori nodded.

"Good. Now as soon as 'our song' ends, you're going to get your purse and we're going to leave." Adam's lips twitched despite his anger. "Our song. The things you think of."

Chapter Seven

Two days later, the house was bustling with activity as it was being readied for Caroline's party. Flowers were arriving, caterers were in the kitchen preparing the food, crates of liquor were delivered. Only Caroline was missing.

Adam came into the living room where Tori was just settling down with a book. "The noise around here is driving me crazy."

"I know," she agreed. "You can't move without bumping into someone."

"How would you like to get out for a little while?"

"And do what?"

"Check on a building I have going up downtown."

"I'd love it." This was the first sign of warmth she'd seen from him since the night she'd met Georgette.

He grabbed her hand and pulled her up off the couch. "Let's go, then."

As they walked into the hall they found Linda standing there arranging some flowers. "Aren't they beautiful?" she asked, slipping a rose in.

Tori paused for a moment and watched the nurse, a frown creasing her forehead. "Come on." Adam tugged on her hand.

When they got outside, he opened the car door for her, then leaned in. "What was wrong back there?"

"I don't know exactly," she said thoughtfully. "Have you ever noticed how Linda always seems to be hovering about whenever something's going on downstairs?"

"No, I can't say that I have. Why?"

"It just makes me uneasy."

Adam reached across Tori and fastened her seat belt, then climbed into the driver's seat.

"What about Sesto?" she asked as Adam put the key in the ignition. "Don't you think he should come with us?"

"I'm tired of having a baby-sitter." He started the engine and they took off.

Tori watched Adam's profile in silence. Something in his attitude told her not to talk. He wanted her company, but he wanted her silent.

The guard saw them coming and opened the gates without stopping them. That was certainly a new experience for Tori.

They drove for miles until they came into the downtown area. He parked on the street in front of a building still under construction. Workers were milling around, undoubtedly on their coffee break. Adam climbed out of the car and looked back at Tori. "Are you coming?"

She quickly climbed out also and followed him to an open elevator that served the construction crew. It looked like nothing more than a mobile crate. Certainly not for the faint of heart.

He held open the gate for her as she ran toward him, then closed it immediately after her. The elevator shot straight up. Tori unconsciously clutched Adam's arm to brace herself. She felt as though she was rising twenty stories without any kind of protection whatsoever.

As Adam looked down at the top of her head, he smiled and protectively wrapped his arm around her slender waist.

When they got to the top of the still wall-less building, Adam raised the gate and walked out. Tori poked her head out first, just to make sure there was at least a floor to stand on. There was.

Adam held out his hand to her. "Come on, Victoria, it's perfectly safe."

"For a cat." She took his hand and stepped out.

"Haven't you ever been in an unfinished building before?"

"Once. When I was five."

Adam looked at her, waiting for an explanation.

"My tree house." She looked around with interested eyes. "So you designed this. I didn't know you were still in the architectural business."

"There are a lot of things you don't know about me."

"Which is something I *do* know."

"Make sure you watch where you walk." Adam went to the open edge and stood with his hands in the pockets of his pants, looking out over the city from his twenty-storey vantage point.

There were very few things that bothered Tori, but being twenty stories up without walls was one of them. It made her a little queasy just to watch him. "Adam?"

"Umm?"

"Would you mind stepping back just a foot or two?"

He turned and looked at her. "Don't you like heights?"

"I love them—when I'm looking up and my feet are planted firmly on the ground."

With a half smile, Adam stepped back and Tori felt better instantly.

"Thank you."

Tori watched him as he walked around checking out the beams and some other things that Tori couldn't put a name to. "Do you miss being an architect?"

"I'm still an architect. I'm simply not a practicing one right now."

"Are you ever going back to it?"

"I'd like to, if anyone will hire me."

"What do you mean?"

"I've got a reputation now. People are going to automatically assume that if someone does business with my company they're doing business with the mob."

"Meaning that they wouldn't be?"

Adam looked at her and a corner of his mouth lifted. "You have more ways of trying to get information than anyone I've ever met."

"I just have a healthy curiosity."

"There's nothing *healthy* about your curiosity, Victoria, trust me."

"So," she continued undaunted, "you left home when you were a teenager. You even went so far as to work your way through school so you wouldn't have to accept money from your family. Why did you come back?"

Adam leaned his shoulder against a steel beam and crossed his arms over his chest. His dark eyes rested on Tori as she ran her fingers over some rivets. "Tell me something."

She looked at him.

"Let's say you were involved in your own life, had a job you loved and responsibilities that needed to be taken care of. Then one day your father called and said he needed you. What would you do?"

"I'd go to my father," she said without hesitation.

"Exactly. You don't turn your back on family, no matter who they are."

"No," she agreed, "you don't."

Adam watched as the wind blew Tori's dark hair across her face. A corner of his mouth lifted as he pushed it away for her.

"What are you thinking?" she asked.

"That you are one of the unlikeliest candidates for an FBI agent that I've ever seen."

"And have you seen many of us?"

"Enough to last me for a while."

She smiled at that. "Describe your version of an agent to me."

"All right." Adam thought for a moment. "Gray three-piece suit, short hair, shoulder holster, and takes him or herself very, very seriously."

She nodded. "I see why I'd give you some problems with that image."

"What made you decide to become an FBI agent?"

"I wonder about that myself at times. I was in college, getting ready to graduate and still unsure about what I wanted to do."

"Liberal arts?"

"Exactly. I was interested in so many different things that I couldn't pinpoint just one course to follow. Then the FBI showed up on campus during a recruiting drive, and as suddenly as that I knew what it was I wanted. Here was a chance to use all the best of what I had. My curiosity," she said with a smile at Adam, "that trait of mine which you find so endearing. Deductive reasoning, negotiating, athletics, imagination. I joined as soon as I graduated."

"And here you are."

"Here I am," she agreed.

"Do you still think it was a good choice?"

"Absolutely." She gazed at Adam. "It's not always easy. Sometimes you lose track of what's right and wrong, and using people becomes a way of life. But if you can keep things in perspective, it makes everything worthwhile."

"What about conflicts of interest?"

"I don't know what you mean."

"Like getting involved with someone you're supposed to be investigating."

"You, for instance?"

"Me."

"Sometimes lately I find the line between what I'm supposed to be doing and what I want to do blurring a little."

"But I'm the bad guy. You're supposed to go after me."

"I'm not convinced."

"I'd think the evidence would be overwhelming by now."

"If it were just facts on paper, I'd want to lock you up and throw away the key. But I'm beginning to know you."

"And?"

"And I think you're a good man, evidence to the contrary."

"It might just be your hormones talking again."

Tori grinned at him. "I'm sure that's part of it, but I have a pretty good handle on them."

"I've noticed." He cupped the back of her head in his hand and looked down at her, his expression tender. "I wish we could have met under different circumstances."

"Is there something in the syndicate's credo about not falling in love with an FBI agent?"

"Not really. I don't think it's ever come up before." His eyes roamed over her face. "You'd be such an easy woman to fall in love with."

"But?"

"But where's the middle ground? Who's going to compromise?" His thumb trailed across the smooth skin of her cheek. He moved her closer. Tori's mouth was inches from his. She looked into his eyes and felt herself melt inside. He was right, of course. There was no middle ground for them.

His mouth brushed against hers, as lightly as the breeze. Tori closed her eyes and then slowly opened them. She raised her hand to his head and tangled her fingers in his hair, pulling his mouth back to hers. Adam's arms went around her, pulling her body closer to his, as his mouth gently captured hers. It was a kiss of exploration rather than possession, and Tori willingly let him inside her inner reaches and then found her way into his.

Adam kissed the corners of her mouth and raised his head so that he could look into her eyes, trying to see what she was feeling. "I think we're in trouble," he said quietly.

Tori rubbed her mouth lightly against his. "That's a distinct possibility."

A strong breeze blew past them at that moment and Tori shivered. Adam opened his jacket and wrapped Tori in its warmth so that she was held securely against him. He rested his mouth against her hair. "I think we should change the subject."

Tori took a deep breath, feeling utter contentment in being here with him. "So, do you like designing office buildings?"

Adam smiled against her hair. "Subtle."

"Thank you."

"Are you really interested?"

"I really am."

He looked around the structure. "Buildings like this are a challenge, but my first love is designing homes."

"Do you follow any particular school of architecture?"

"Frank Lloyd Wright, more than any other. I like to design homes that blend into the landscape rather than compete with it. And I like to design the furniture. I'll have to show you my home sometime."

"Your home?" She hadn't seen anything in his file that indicated he lived anywhere other than in the compound.

"It's in the country. My closest neighbor is more than ten miles away."

"I'd like to see it."

"Mr. Danaro!" a man called as he climbed off the elevator, blueprints in his hand. "I'm glad you stopped by today. There are some things I need to clear with you."

Adam moved Tori away from him and smiled down at her as he took off his jacket and draped it over her shoulders. "You look cold," he explained, then walked away from her.

Tori pulled the ends of the jacket together to keep the wind out and walked away from Adam and as close to the edge as she dared—which wasn't very close—and looked out over the city.

The men must have finished their break because things were starting to buzz back to life in the building. There was the sound of metal hammering against metal and the hum of the heavy equipment below as steel beams were raised into place. Tori could hear men shouting at one another and laughing.

Tori turned and watched Adam. He was leaning over the blueprints, explaining something to the man who'd brought them. A group of workers passed her and she stepped slightly back to make room for them. As she turned to make sure she wasn't too close to the edge, something or someone hit her in the middle of her back, propelling her forward. "Adam!" she screamed as she grabbed at something, anything to stop her from going over the edge.

Adam looked up just as she went over the side. "No!" he yelled as he raced to the edge and looked down. Tori was dangling twenty stories in the air, her hands gripping an overhanging beam that she'd caught on her way over the edge, about three feet below the ledge. The jacket she'd had over her shoulders fluttered to earth. Adam went down onto his stomach and braced himself, but no matter how he stretched, he couldn't reach her.

"Oh, God," she cried, "I can't hang on. My arms—"

Adam couldn't let himself feel anything yet. "Hold on. Just hold on. I'll be right there." He looked at the men who were standing there watching. "Four of you grab my legs and lower me over the side. As soon as I have her, pull me up."

Tori closed her eyes and tried not to think about the pain shooting through her arms, or the aching tiredness in her hands. Her fingers slipped a little and she screamed again.

"Victoria, open your eyes."

She did, and found herself looking at Adam.

"I'm going to grab you by your wrists. As soon as I do, let go of the beam. Okay, let's do it." He wrapped his strong hands around her wrists and Tori, with complete faith in him, let go. The sudden addition of her weight threw the men holding onto Adam off-balance and both Adam and Tori dropped lower.

She looked down, and terror filled her. She tried to get some control over her breathing to calm herself down, but it wasn't helping much. *I will not faint,* she told herself. *I will not faint.* If she did, she'd just be deadweight and that would make things worse. She looked at the hands holding her wrists. The veins on Adam's arms were standing out from the effort he was making. His eyes locked with hers.

"It's going to be all right. Just don't look down."

Suddenly there was some movement. She could hear the grunts of the men as they pulled Adam up. And then lots of hands were grabbing her arms and pulling her over the edge and back into the safety of the building.

She fell onto Adam, who wrapped her in his arms and held her as though he'd never let her go. Both of them were breathing hard. Tori's eyes suddenly filled with tears. Adam pressed her face into his shoulder. "You're all right now. Everything's all right. Can you tell me what happened?"

She shook her head and put her hand at her throat. "I think I'm going to be sick."

"Sit up and put your head between your legs."

She did, and Adam stayed with her, his hand gently stroking the back of her neck.

"Concentrate on your breathing," he said gently, feeling a little sick himself. "You're hyperventilating. Take fewer breaths. You're safe now." Then he looked at the men standing around watching. "Did any of you see what happened?"

They all shook their heads.

"I want you to call the police to get a statement from everyone who was present," he told the man he'd been speaking to when Tori went over the edge. "I want to know what happened."

Then he looked back at Tori. "Are you all right?" he asked, still stroking the back of her neck.

She took a shaky breath and nodded. "I think so."

"I'm taking you to the hospital."

"I'm fine. Or at least I will be."

Adam rose and took Tori's hand in his to help her to her feet. She got about halfway up and her knees buckled beneath her, she was trembling so badly.

"Do you hurt anywhere?"

"My ribs. I hit myself on that beam when I fell."

Without hesitation, he scooped her into his arms and carried her to the elevator. One of the men opened the door for them. "Call the hospital," Adam told him. "Tell them what happened and to be ready for us."

Tori hated being this weak, but there wasn't anything she could do about it. For once she just let someone else take care of things.

From the time he put her in the car until they parked in the hospital's emergency entrance was a matter of about ten minutes. Two orderlies came out with a bed that they lifted her carefully onto, then wheeled her into the emergency room while Adam walked beside her holding her hand.

Then they came to a point where they asked Adam to wait outside while they wheeled her between two double steel doors. A doctor came and checked her over, then sent her down for X rays. The doctor called Adam in before he even spoke to Tori. "You," he looked at Tori, "have two bruised ribs. Badly bruised. I'll wrap you up here and I can send you home tonight, but you're going to need rest. The nurse is getting you some pain pills, and they should help, but rest is still the best thing." Then he looked at Adam. "How did this happen?"

"She fell off of a building."

The doctor arched an eyebrow. "Well, that's a first for me."

"It was a first for her, too."

"And a last," Tori chimed in.

Adam walked over to Tori and kissed the top of her head. "I have to fill out some medical forms while the doctor tapes your ribs. I'll be right back."

When the doctor had finished with her, Tori gingerly managed to sit up. A nurse who was cleaning up after the doctor handed Tori her blouse from the back of a chair. Tori got her arms through it, but her hands were still shaking so badly it was difficult to button.

Adam came in and gently brushed her trembling hands away to finish the job himself. "Come on," he said as he helped her to her feet. "Let's go home."

He settled her into the car and then started the drive back to the house. Tori studied his profile as he drove. He seemed preoccupied. "What are you thinking?"

He shook his head and didn't say anything.

"Adam, what's wrong?"

He looked at her and then back at the road. "You almost died today."

"But I didn't."

"It was too close."

"It was an accident. One of the men bumped into me."

"Then why didn't he say so?"

"Maybe he was frightened because of what nearly happened."

"I don't think so. Those men are all experienced construction workers. What happened to you today just doesn't happen accidentally. They would have known better than to bump you."

"Well, it certainly could not have been a planned accident. No one knew we were going there. You didn't even know yourself until moments before we left the house."

"I go there several times a week."

"But I've never been there before. No one would have been expecting me to show up."

Adam was silent for the rest of the drive. When they got home, he started to carry her upstairs, but she gently pushed his hands aside. "I can walk. My ribs are bruised, not my legs."

It was a slow trip, but she made it. The pain pills were starting to do their work, and by the time she got to the bedroom Tori was exhausted. She sank onto the edge of the bed with a sigh.

"Are you all right?" Adam asked.

She nodded.

"Where do you keep your pajamas?"

"In the middle drawer."

He pulled out the first nightgown he found. It was another soft white cotton one with lace around the bottom and at the throat. He tossed it over the foot of the bed, then bent over Tori and started to unbutton her blouse.

She put her hand over his. "I can do it."

"You can, with difficulty. I, on the other hand, can do it quickly and with ease."

She left her hand over his.

"Come on," he coaxed. "I've seen one or two women's bodies in my time. Besides, even if I like what I see, you're in no condition to let me do anything about it."

Tori smiled and moved her hand. Adam undressed her with practiced hands, slid the nightgown over her head and buttoned it up the back. After settling her against the pillows, he looked down at her and smoothed her hair away from her face. "How do your ribs feel?"

"I know they're there," she said wryly. "I can't imagine why I didn't notice that I'd hurt myself sooner."

"It was the adrenaline."

She took a deep breath and winced. Her eyes rested on the top of Adam's head as he picked up her clothes. "Thank you for coming after me the way you did."

"Did you think I was just going to leave you there?"

"I don't know what I thought. I mean, you've found me to be quite an annoyance lately."

He smiled at her. "Would you like me to stay with you until you fall asleep?"

She would have loved it, but hated to show that kind of weakness. "That's nice of you, but no. I'm really fine now."

Adam sat on the edge of the bed and took her hand in his. "You're stuck with me anyway." He leaned over and kissed her forehead. "Get some rest."

"You don't have to do this, you know."

"I'm not here with you because I have to be, Victoria. If you don't know that by now, you should."

A shy smile touched her mouth. "Thank you."

Adam watched as her eyes slowly drifted closed, and shook his head. "You try so hard to be tough when in reality you're so gentle," he said softly.

There was a knock on the door and Adam quietly crossed the room to answer it. Salvatore frowned up at him from his wheelchair. "What's this I hear about Tori being hurt? What happened?"

Adam stepped aside so his grandfather could enter. He wheeled himself over to the bed and looked at the sleeping woman. "Is she all right?"

"She will be." Adam sank into a chair facing the bed. "The trick is going to be keeping her safe."

"What are you talking about?"

"She was pushed off the twentieth floor of a building this afternoon."

Salvatore looked at him in horror. "My God."

"That's putting it mildly. It's only by the slimmest piece of luck that she's alive."

"Could it have been an accident?"

"I don't think so."

"But why? Why would anyone want to hurt her?"

"For one of two reasons: either someone knows who she really is or it was intended as an object lesson for me."

"But how could anyone have known where you'd be?"

"I don't know. Yet."

"Are you going to send her back to Washington?"

"I can't. If I do, her boss will be all over us. We can't afford to have him nosing around right now. He could blow everything."

Salvatore studied his grandson for a long moment. "You're pale," he finally concluded.

Adam's eyes rested quietly on Tori. "If anything had happened to her..."

Salvatore nodded. "She's in love with you, you know."

Adam didn't say anything.

"Maybe you should just tell her what's going on."

"I can't do that. It puts her in too awkward a position. She's already caught between her work and me. I don't want to make it any worse for her."

"Mr. Danaro?" His nurse looked into the room. "You really should be getting back to bed."

Salvatore reached out and squeezed Adam's shoulder. "It'll all work out. You'll see."

Adam nodded in silence.

Chapter Eight

W ell."

Tori opened her eyes to find Caroline standing next to her bed, her hands on her hips.

"If you didn't want to come to my party, all you had to do was say so. Falling off a building is a little extreme just to get out of an invitation."

Tori smiled sleepily at her. "I'm really sorry about that."

Caroline sat on the edge of the bed. "So am I. Are you all right?"

"I'll be fine in a few days."

"Grandfather said it was close."

She struggled a little to sit up. Caroline leaned over and propped up some pillows for her. "Has the party started yet?'' Tori asked, noticing the lovely dress her sister-in-law was wearing.

"The music is playing, but no guests are here yet. They should start arriving in about ten minutes."

"Is my not being there going to be a problem for you?"

Caroline smiled at her. "Oh, I think we'll be able to find something or other to celebrate. Besides, Adam promised he'd make an appearance. Wait until you see him. He's one of the best-looking men I've ever seen in a tuxedo, even if he is my own brother."

"Where is he?"

"I don't know. He left the house a little while ago and said he'd be right back."

A doorbell chimed below.

"And the party begins," Caroline said with a sigh as she rose from the bed. "You get some rest and we'll talk tomorrow."

"Have a good party."

Caroline winked at her as she softly closed the bedroom door.

Tori lay there staring at the ceiling. Her fingers drummed against the sheets. Where was Adam?

Adam was standing in front of a door, waiting for someone to answer his ring.

Georgette Lowell answered finally and looked at him in surprise. "Adam? What's going on? Is Angelo expecting you?"

Adam walked past her. "No. Where is he?"

"Well, he's in his office, but I—"

"I'll announce myself."

Georgette, a curious frown creasing her forehead, closed the heavy wood door and stood in the hallway staring after him.

Adam walked into the office and stood there. Angelo, who was on the phone, hung up abruptly and got to his feet. "What the hell is going on here?"

"You and I are about to have a talk."

Angelo pressed something under his desk and Adam smiled. It was a menacing smile. "If your intention is to get Bruno in here to rescue you, forget it. He's outside enjoying Sesto's company."

"Listen, Danaro—"

"No, you listen, Fortuna, and listen carefully. Sit down."

Angelo did. Tiny beads of sweat broke out on his forehead.

Adam, palms flat on the desk, leaned toward him. "My wife was nearly killed today, but something tells me you already know all about that."

"What would I know about that?"

"Nothing. Just like you don't know anything about how Brian got killed."

Angelo licked dry lips.

"I'm going to tell you right now that if anything happens to Victoria—and I mean anything—if she should meet with any kind of accident; if she should catch a cold; if one hair on her head gets mussed, I'll know who to come looking for. Do I make myself clear?"

"You've got me wrong, man. I wouldn't hurt her."

"Answer the question, Angelo. Have I made myself clear?"

"Yeah, yeah."

"Good." Adam straightened away from the desk. "Then we understand each other. And one other thing."

Angelo waited.

"Negotiations on the hotel stock are over. If you want it, you'd better come up with fifteen million dollars in cash in one week."

"One week? It can't be done!"

"Then I'll sell it to someone else. One week, Angelo."

He left the office and went down the hall. "Goodbye, Georgette," he said politely as he passed her in the hallway and went out the front door.

She walked down to where her lover was. "Angelo? What was that about?"

"Get out of here and close the door," he said angrily.

She did, and stood in the hallway, frowning.

Tori heard the music coming from downstairs and the steady hum of conversation. It sounded like everyone was having a nice time. And here she was.

She sighed and looked around. There wasn't even a good book to read. She sat up straighter, trying not to take too deep a breath, and managed to do it without hurting herself too much. From there it was a short distance to standing, which hurt a little more, but wasn't anything she couldn't handle. Walking was a piece of cake compared to standing and she made it across the room to the closet. Hanging in there was a sapphire-blue silk dress with a boat neck and long sleeves. The waist was dropped to below her hips and then flared out. She'd bought it in Paris the day she was there with Adam, and hadn't worn it since her one night with him.

It was, luckily, an easy dress to get into, though her panty hose required a little more effort because of the bending. As she looked at herself in the mirror, she shook her head. Something wasn't right. Her hair was too casual for the dress.

Reaching into her drawer, she pulled out a rhinestone studded banana clip, brushed her hair straight back except for the light ruffle of bangs and caught it in the clip.

With a little makeup, she was ready to go.

"What do you think you're doing?"

Startled, Tori turned to find Adam standing in the doorway watching her. "Don't sneak up on me like that."

"Sorry." He moved farther into the room. "But the question still stands. What are you doing?"

"I'm going to a party."

"The doctor said you were supposed to rest."

"And I have."

"So now you're all better?"

"No, of course not. But I was bored and I really don't hurt all that much. I thought maybe I could go down for just a little while." Her eyes moved over

Adam, immaculate in his tuxedo. "You look wonderful."

"So do you." His eyes moved down the length of her body in a particularly intimate way. "I remember the dress."

"Thank you."

"Wait there a moment. I'll be right back."

"But—"

"Just wait."

He left the room and Tori turned back to the mirror to dab on a little more lipstick.

He came back in just a few minutes with a long, black velvet case. Tori looked from it to Adam. "What's that?"

"Something I bought for you in Paris to go with the dress." He pressed the catch and the lid flew open to reveal a delicate two strand diamond and sapphire necklace and matching earrings.

"Oh, Adam," she breathed, "you didn't."

"Quite obviously, I did," he said, taking out the necklace. "Turn around and face the mirror."

Tori followed his instructions.

Adam's hands came over her head as he gently lay the necklace against her throat and fastened it from behind.

"There," he said, his hands warm on the back of her neck. "What do you think?"

Tori fingered the brilliant stones. "It's beautiful." She met his mirrored gaze. "But I can't accept something like this."

"I had a feeling you'd say that. Just wear it tonight, then. And the earrings."

She lifted them carefully out of the box and fastened them to her ears. "What do you think?" she asked turning toward him.

He stood back to look at the overall effect. "I think," he said quietly, "that you are the most beautiful woman I've ever seen."

"And I have great posture," she said with smile, lightening things between them.

"Excuse me?"

"The way my ribs are wrapped is like wearing a corset. I couldn't slouch if I wanted to."

"Do you want to?"

"Want to what?"

"Slouch."

"No."

"Good." He held out his arm for her. "Then you're all set."

She put her hand on his arm, and for the first time Adam saw her wrist. He picked it up in his hand and looked at the terrible bruising. "Did I do this to you?"

"Yes. And thank you. Bruises are far preferable to the alternative."

He raised her wrist to his mouth and kissed the delicate underside. "I'm sorry."

His mouth against her skin sent a physical wave through Tori. She gently removed her hand from his and placed it on his arm. "I'm ready when you are."

"That's not the impression I get."

A smile tugged at her mouth. "I meant for Caroline's party."

"Ah. Well, let's go then."

Caroline spotted them when they were halfway down the stairs and raced up to meet them. "What are you doing?" she chastised Tori. "I was only kidding earlier. You shouldn't be up yet."

"I know you were kidding, but everyone sounded like they were having so much fun, I couldn't just lie there and feel sorry for myself when I could be down here having fun."

"Well put," Adam complimented her.

"Thank you."

Caroline shook her head. "Personally, I think you're both crazy, but then who am I to judge?"

"Who are you, indeed?" Adam couldn't resist. "Don't forget that I've known you your entire life, and what Tori's doing can't hold a candle to most of your stunts. Although," he looked down at his wife, "she's giving you some competition in some other areas."

Tori smiled innocently up at him. "Shall we dance?"

"Let's negotiate the rest of the stairs first."

It took some time, but with Caroline on one side and Adam on the other, she made it.

"Everyone!" Caroline interrupted her guests' chatter. "Please, everyone. I'd like all of you to meet my new sister-in-law, Victoria Danaro. Victoria," she finished the introduction, "this is everyone. Meet them as you mingle."

Adam tried to stay with her, but somewhere along the way they got separated. Tori looked up once in a while and her eyes unerringly found him. Despite her light manner lately, she knew that there was some pain coming her way. He was right about that middle ground. They didn't have any, and without it, no relationship could survive.

After about an hour and a half, she was really tired. This time when she looked up, it was right into Adam's eyes. He excused himself and crossed the room. "Are you all right?" he asked quietly.

"I'm a little tired."

"Come on, then. I'll take you to bed."

"Not yet."

"But, you said—"

"I'd like to go outside for a minute."

Adam took her arm and looked down at her. "Are you sure you're all right?"

"I'm sure. Really. I just want some fresh air."

As soon as they got outside, Adam took off his jacket and draped it across her shoulders. "I don't think I have even a minute of small talk left in me," he said as they walked across the compound to the Sound.

"I know what you mean, but it's been fun."

Adam looked down at a bench facing the water. "Can you sit down?"

"Sure." Tori took her time, keeping her torso erect, as she slowly sank onto the bench, letting out a long breath when she was finally settled. "There."

Adam shook his head as he sat next to her. "You should be in bed."

"I bet you say that to all the girls."

Adam laughed, then grew quiet.

"Where were you earlier?" Tori asked. "Caroline said you left the compound."

"Do I have to check in with you now?"

"No more than I do with you."

"All right. I went to see Angelo Fortuna."

"No!"

"Yes!"

"What did you say to him?"

"I told him that negotiations for the hotel stock were over. That if he wanted it he was going to have to come up with the cash within the week."

"And what did he say?"

"That it was impossible."

"And what did you say?"

"That he'd better come up with it or I'd sell it to someone who could."

"Then what did he say?"

"Nothing. That was the end of our conversation, thank heavens. I feel as though I've been relating a conversational Ping-Pong ball."

"Do you think he'll do it?"

"I have no idea."

"Maybe you should have given him more time."

"I'm tired of playing his little cat-and-mouse game. I want to get this thing over with so I can move on to other things."

"Meaning you want me out of here," she guessed quietly.

"That's part of it," he agreed. "You're not safe here."

"Are you?"

"I can take care of myself."

"That's what I used to think."

Adam looked at her curiously. "Don't you anymore?"

"Honestly?"

"Honestly."

"That fall over the side of the building shook my confidence. I couldn't have foreseen that happening, and once it did I couldn't do anything to stop it. Nothing that uncontrollable has ever happened to me before." She thought for a moment. "Except for the way I feel about you, of course."

Adam put his arm around her shoulders and drew her closer to him. "Those pain pills have loosened your tongue."

Tori sighed. "I suppose."

"Do you think they've loosened anything else?"

Tori jabbed him in the side and smiled. "This is a side of you I've never seen before."

"I'm full of sides you've never seen."

Still in the circle of his arm, Tori looked up at him. "Do you think I ever will?"

"I don't know, sweetheart." He kissed the top of her head. "I just don't know. Things aren't looking too promising so far."

Chapter Nine

One week later, Tori stood in the upstairs hallway and looked down at the driveway. Angelo Fortuna was getting out of his limousine. Almost as though he knew she was watching, he looked up and right at her. Tori didn't move, but met his look head-on. Little did he know he was coming to the end of his career in crime.

Her face gave nothing away until he was safely inside the house. Then she allowed herself a smile.

"Mrs. Danaro?"

She turned to find Salvatore's nurse standing behind her.

"Mr. Danaro would like to see you."

"Of course." She walked down the hall to his room and looked inside. "Hello, there."

He smiled weakly. "Come in, dear."

She tried not to look as sad as she felt at his obviously worsening condition. "How are you feeling?"

"Fine. A little tired, though. What's going on downstairs?"

"What makes you think anything is?"

"I've lived in this house a lot of years. There's something in the air today."

"You have good instincts."

"I know. That's why I'm still around."

"Well, as a matter of fact, Angelo Fortuna is downstairs closing a business transaction with Adam."

Salvatore smiled with satisfaction. "Ahh."

Tori looked at Linda, who seemed to be finding an inordinate amount of busy work around the room. "Would you excuse us, please?"

The nurse looked up in surprise. "Me? Oh, of course. I'm sorry. I'll come back in a little while."

She left the room but didn't close the door, so Tori got up and closed it.

"Don't you trust her?"

Tori shook her head as she returned to her seat. "I'm not sure."

"Any particular reason?"

"No."

He looked thoughtfully at the closed door, then set it aside. "So tell me, what exactly is happening?"

"I think maybe Adam should be the one to tell you."

Salvatore looked at her with kindly eyes. "You can talk to me. I know who you are, Tori."

Her eyes met his, unsure of what to say.

"I've known since not long after you showed up.'

"You had me checked out?"

"From head to toe. And Adam confirmed it."

"So you know we're married—but not really *married*."

"I know you're in love with each other. That's been obvious since the first day."

She leaned back in her chair and smiled at him. "You're something."

"Thank you. So, are we nailing Angelo with this little deal?"

She nodded. "It looks like it. Of course, it'll take at least a year to get him behind bars. Courts take forever, particularly in tax matters."

"And what about for Brian's murder?"

"I'm afraid we haven't found anything yet, but I'm still hoping something will break."

There was a knock on the door and Adam walked in. He looked at Tori and smiled. "Got him. He just doesn't know it yet."

"He will, as soon as I call it in and the IRS starts doing its job."

He looked at Salvatore. "Will you excuse us, Grandfather? I need to talk to Victoria for a minute."

Tori walked into the hallway with him. "What's wrong?"

"I'm still worried about Angelo. This whole set-up could blow up in our faces."

"No, it won't. You've hooked him. All the IRS has to do is reel him in."

"And in the meantime he's still out there, walking around."

"So?"

"I don't trust him."

"Of course you don't. No one in his right mind would."

"He's going to know as soon as he's contacted by the IRS that he was set up, and he's going to know by whom."

"Not necessarily. It's an enormous purchase. The IRS would naturally be interested in it."

"Victoria, he's going to know. And he's going to try to get back at me. The best way for him to do that is through you."

"He wouldn't."

"I've seen him in action, Victoria. I know what he's capable of. You're going to have to trust my judgment on this."

"What are you telling me?"

"You got what you came for. Now it's time for you to leave."

Her eyes searched his. "You can't mean that."

Adam's expression grew tender. "I want you out of harm's way. I've always wanted you out of harm's way. I think this whole scheme of Parker's was off-balance to begin with. There was no need for you to be here at all.''

''Charlie just wanted to keep you honest.''

''And what could you have done about it if I hadn't been?''

''Told him.''

''Would you?''

''I guess I'm just lucky that I didn't have to find out.''

''I guess we both are.''

''I still have an idea about Brian . . .''

Adam shook his head. ''No. Enough is enough. I want you to go back to Washington.''

''Back to Washington?''

''That's where your home is. That's where your work is. It's where you belong. Not Connecticut.''

''But what about you? Are you going to stay here?''

''Yes.''

''Just like that?''

''Just like that,'' he replied.

''For how long?''

''As long as it takes.''

''As long as what takes?'' she asked, a trifle desperately.

''Some business dealings I have going on right now.''

''Maybe I can help you with them.''

''Victoria, you're not hearing me. I want you to leave here.''

''But I don't want to leave you,'' she said quietly.

"You don't have a choice. Neither of us has."

"That's it?"

"You go back to Washington and fall in love with a nice FBI agent."

"Don't patronize me."

The muscle in his jaw moved. "I'm sorry, but this thing between us—it's no good. It won't work."

"It could be wonderful if we'd just give it a chance."

He shook his head. "You're so rational about everything else, but you can't see the obvious when it comes to us."

"The only thing obvious about us is that we're in love and have been for a very long time. I let my job get in the way once before and I don't want to make that mistake again."

"It's not just your job, Victoria. It's your way of life versus mine. I'm locked into a world completely foreign to you right now, and I'm going to be locked into it for quite a while longer."

"I'm not going to sit in judgment of you. I did that once before and it was a terrible mistake."

"No," he disagreed. "You were reasoning with your mind then, not your heart. Your first instincts were the right ones."

"Adam," she said quietly, "don't do this. Don't throw me away like this."

"Oh, Tori," he said, for the first time using her nickname, "I'm not throwing you away. All I'm trying to do is what's right for both of us."

"What's right for me is to be with you."

"No." He shook his head. "What's right for you is to go back to your life in Washington and get on with things there."

She looked at him in silence. "You've already made up your mind, haven't you?" she finally asked. "It doesn't matter what arguments I use with you now because the decision has been made that I don't belong here."

He nodded.

Tori's throat closed with emotion. She couldn't have spoken if she'd wanted to. Without looking at him again, she went into their bedroom and began packing her suitcases. She didn't expect Adam to follow her, and he didn't.

It didn't take much time. When she was finished, she carried them down herself, hardly noticing the ache in her side. She stood in front of Adam's office door, her hand poised to knock, but she stopped. It was several seconds before she got enough of a grip on herself to be sure she wouldn't cry in front of him.

Taking a deep breath, she raised her hand and knocked firmly.

"Come in."

She opened the door and walked in. "I'm packed and ready to go. I'd appreciate it if you'd call the front gate and tell them to let me through."

His eyes rested on her for a long moment before he said anything. As always, he was impossible to read. "All right. Have a safe trip back."

"Thank you." She lightly cleared her throat. "I didn't say goodbye to Salvatore. I'd appreciate it if you'd do that for me. Tell him that I'll write and call."

"I will."

"And Mrs. Rosetti and Caroline. I guess that's all."

"Goodbye, Victoria," he said quietly.

She swallowed hard. "Goodbye. I, uh—" she cleared her throat again "—I wish you all the best."

When she'd gone, Adam sat behind his desk and tiredly rubbed his forehead. Why was it that knowing he was doing the right thing didn't make it any less painful?

"Tori?"

She looked up from the file she was working on to the secretary she shared with another agent.

"Line two. She wouldn't give her name."

"Thanks, Sue." She pressed the flashing button on her phone and picked up the receiver. "Agent Burton speaking."

"Victoria? This is Georgette Lowell."

"Georgette?" she asked in surprise.

"Yeah. I need to talk to you. It's important."

"Where are you now?"

"I'm down the street at some hamburger place."

"Do you want me to meet you there, or would you rather come here?"

"I'll meet you in your office."

"Georgette? Are you all right?"

"I will be."

Tori hung up the phone and thoughtfully tapped the eraser end of a pencil on a legal pad. What was going on? And how did Georgette know how to get in touch with her?

With a little shake of her head, Tori went back to the file she'd been working on and finished the notation she'd started.

"Tori?"

She turned at her secretary's voice to find Georgette standing there. "Thanks, Sue. Close the door behind you, please."

Georgette looked around the little office. "So, you really are an FBI agent. Mind if I sit down?"

Tori waved her into a chair across from her desk. "How did you find out who I was?"

"I overheard Angelo talking to Salvatore's nurse. Linda, I think her name is."

So Linda had been listening in on conversations after all!

"You don't have to worry about her anymore," Georgette hastened to add. "Adam fired her a few months ago. Not long after you left, as a matter of fact. She's living with Angelo now."

"She's living with . . . What about you?"

"He kicked me out." Georgette snapped her fingers. "Just like that. But I'm going to have the last laugh."

"What are you talking about?"

"I have something that belongs to him."

"What?"

She reached into her purse and pulled out a gun wrapped in Saran Wrap. "This," she said as she set it on the desk.

Tori looked from the gun to Georgette. "Where did you get this?"

"Does it matter?"

"Yes, it does. Very much."

"Angelo has a safe hidden in the house. I watched him open it once when he didn't know I was looking. I went back in there when I finally figured out that he was going to replace me with Linda, and this is what I found. Actually, I found a lot of things, but putting two and two together, with you and Adam, and knowing about Adam's brother, I thought this might tell some tales."

Tori nodded. "Thank you. I'll have it checked out."

Georgette looked near to tears. "Good. I hope you find something. I hope it turns out to be the gun. And I'll tell you something else, Victoria—I know for a fact that he hit Brian Danaro himself."

"How?"

"He told me one night. He was a little high and I guess he was still worried about impressing me back then."

"Would you be willing to make a statement to that effect under oath?"

"You bet I would."

Tori didn't know how much weight it would carry, considering the vindictive nature of such a statement coming from her, but every little bit helped.

"I overheard something else. Linda was the one who told him you'd be in that building the day you went there with Adam. Angelo sent someone in, and that someone pushed you."

"But why?"

"For the simple reason that he hates Adam Danaro. He's always hated him. Hurting you was an easy way for him to get to Adam."

Tori looked at the gun again, then signaled her secretary through the glass wall to come in. "Sue, I want to take this gun to ballistics and get it tested for comparison with the bullets used in the murder of Brian Danaro."

The secretary carefully picked up up. "How soon do you need the information?"

"As soon as they can get it to me."

"I'll tell them."

Tori leaned back in her chair and studied the woman across from her. "Anything else?"

"Just a little advice. If you have any influence with Adam at all, tell him to watch out. Angelo's mad."

"Are you taking your own advice?"

"You know it. I'm getting as far away from Connecticut as I can go."

"Keep in touch, though, so we know where to reach you."

"First you arrest him, then I'll tell you where I am."

"What about your statement?"

"I'll make that now."

"All right. I'll get someone in here to take it down."

"Is this going to take long? I have a plane to catch."

"Maybe an hour."

Georgette looked at Tori and exhaled a long breath. "I'm scared, but it feels good. Revenge really is sweet."

The next morning, Tori sat at her desk reading the ballistic and fingerprint reports. She reached for her telephone and pressed Adam's phone number. She had to go through two people before she finally reached him, but the minute she heard his voice, her heart started its familiar hammering.

"Hello, Adam, this is Tori."

"Victoria? Is everything all right?"

"It's fine. Actually, it's more than fine. I was calling to tell you that we've got possession of the gun that killed Brian. It belongs to Angelo Fortuna. He was picked up earlier this morning and charged."

There was silence for a moment. "Thank you."

"You don't sound pleased."

"I am. It's just the timing. Salvatore died early this morning."

Quick tears sprang to Tori's eyes. "Oh, Adam, I'm so sorry. Is there anything I can do?"

"Not really. He was ready."

"Would you like me to come—"

"No." He cut her off. "I'd rather you didn't."

"All right."

"Thank you for calling, Victoria. I appreciate it."

"I thought you'd like to know."

"Goodbye."

"Bye." Tori hung up the phone and stared at it. Once again she was left feeling helpless.

Chapter Ten

Snap.

Tori looked away from her office window to find her boss standing in the doorway snapping his fingers.

"Working hard I see," he remarked as he entered and sat in a chair across from her.

"I was thinking."

"About what?"

"About me." She studied him for a minute. "If you had to describe my personality in one word, what would it be?"

Charlie grinned at her. "Your personality couldn't possibly be described in anything less than ten words."

"Determined," she said as though she hadn't heard him. "I'm a very determined person."

"That's definitely one of the ten words I would use."

"And for months I've been shockingly undetermined."

"Shockingly?"

"Shockingly."

"This sounds serious." He was getting interested now. "In what way have you wimped out?"

"Wimped out. That's a good word for it."

"Thank you."

"You're welcome." She got up and began pacing back and forth. "There is a man out there I'm in love with, and I just let him go."

"No."

"Yes."

"Would the man by any chance be Adam Danaro?"

"That's right."

Charlie wasn't amused anymore. "He's not for you, Tori. The guy is bad news."

"You don't know him."

"I know about him, and that's enough. And if it's taken you all of this time to figure things out, then you already know he's bad news."

"It's taken me all of this time to figure out that when he sent me away, it wasn't because he wanted to. It was because he felt he had to."

"He sent you away? Doesn't that tell you anything?"

"It tells me that he loves me."

"You're dreaming."

"I don't think so."

"A relationship with Danaro could cost you your job."

"I know that."

"Don't you care?"

"Of course I care." She stopped pacing and looked down at Charlie. "But he's more important to me than this job."

"What's this? Another sudden realization?"

"I guess so."

Charlie exhaled a long breath. "So what now?"

"I'm going to go talk to him."

"And if he rejects you again?"

"I don't know. I'll have to worry about that when the time comes."

"That's not very pragmatic."

"No, I suppose it's not."

"Then again, that's never stopped you before."

She wasn't listening. "Charlie, may I have a few days off?"

Charlie seemed to be going through some inner battle. "I would love to be able to say no, but you haven't even taken your vacation time for last year. Starting when?"

"This afternoon."

He shook his head. "You're making a mistake, Tori."

"Maybe," she said quietly, "but I've made them before and survived to tell about them."

"This is different."

Tori took her purse out of her drawer, then leaned over and kissed Charlie on the top of his head. "I'll be all right."

As soon as Tori got home, she tried to call Adam, but a woman whose voice she didn't know answered the phone and told her that Adam was away for the week.

Undaunted, she remembered that Adam had said something about having his own isolated home, and she called someone she knew at the IRS to check on whether or not Adam had deducted property taxes and if so, for what address. He had, also in Connecticut, and Tori was on her way.

It had been warmer in the day and the snow had begun to melt, but now the slush that had been created was starting to freeze and snow was falling again. Rather than drive in that kind of weather, Tori went to the airport and bought a ticket for a commuter flight.

And she waited. And she waited. That flight got canceled and they scheduled her for another one. And she waited. And she waited.

That one finally boarded three hours late. The flight made two stops before landing in Connecticut. That meant she had to sit through three takeoffs and three landings, which were not her strong point when it came to flying—particularly when you couldn't see your hand in front of your face.

Once she got to the airport in Connecticut, she went straight to a car rental agency, only to discover that all of the sturdy cars had been taken. She ended up with something small and light—just what everyone needed on a snowy night.

From there she went to the baggage claim area and was told that her luggage had somehow mistakenly been taken off the plane at another stop and wouldn't be at the airport until the next day.

She shook her head as she went outside to pick up her car. This wasn't going well. It wasn't going well at all.

Once she got settled into the car, she pulled out a map and studied it. Adam's home was about an hour from the airport. It didn't look difficult to find.

Wrong.

Because of the weather, what should have been an easy drive turned into a nightmare. She was already two hours into the one-hour drive when she heard something like a shot and suddenly the little car swerved out of control on the ice. She managed to slide to a stop on the side of the road, knowing exactly what she was going to find before she even got out of the car. Turning on her flashing lights, she unbuckled her seat belt and stepped out into snow and slush that covered her boots halfway up to her knees. Trudging through it, squinting against the driving snow to the back of the car, she saw the flat tire. She looked at it, shaking her head. What else could happen?

She should never have asked that question. A semi-trailer sped by at that moment, its huge wheels churning through the muck on the road. "Oh, no!" she yelled as she saw it coming, and tried desperately to back out of the way. But she wasn't fast enough. The last tire to pass her sent a river of slush flying through the air, most of which landed on the front of her coat. She stood there looking down at herself, then she looked at the car. Without saying anything, she trudged back to it and kicked the flat tire.

Feeling a little better, she dug through the trunk and found everything she needed to change a tire, then stood back and looked at what she'd gathered. "Now, if only I knew what to do with you. There must be instructions around here someplace." She dug around some more, then noticed a piece of paper that had been pasted to the inner trunk lid. By this time it was nearly dark out and her only light came from a little bulb inside the trunk. Squinting to read, she saw a picture of a car and a jack. "All right! This is it." Leaning farther in, her eyes made out some of the words. "How to Use the Jack. See instruction book." She sighed. "Great. What instruction book?" Her eyes moved onto the next item. "Warning: never crawl under a car when it is jacked up. The jack screw should be well greased and free from dirt." Tori shook her head. "Right. I'll just take care of that immediately." She leaned farther into the trunk. "First apply the hand brake and engage the gear or P position." Tori made her way to the driver's side of the car and made sure she'd already done that, then went back to the trunk. "A jack socket anchorage is situated by each wheel. Car and jack should be on a firm flat surface." Tori looked down at the snow and slush and shook her head. "Place the jack and insert jack arm in socket anchorage next to wheel to be raised." Tori took out everything she needed and followed the instructions she could up to that point. Leaning back into the car, she read some more. "Make sure the jack arm is pushed well into the socket anchorage." And then there was a series of pictures that showed her what to do.

The snow made it difficult. She had to dig around the tire so that when she got the vehicle jacked up, she could slide one tire off and the other on. By the time she was finished, her fingers were freezing, but the job was done. Climbing back into the car, she turned on the overhead light and glanced into the rearview mirror. "Oh, no," she groaned. Her hair was plastered against her head. There was a great streak of dirt on her nose and cheek, and when she tried to wipe them off with her hand, she just made them worse because her hands were so greasy. Holding them away from her much the way a doctor does after he's scrubbed, she looked around for something to wipe on, and ended up using the only tissue she'd brought with her which, needless to say, didn't do much good. Gingerly putting her hands on the steering wheel, she tried to move the car forward. The rear wheels spun, but nothing happened. She was stuck.

Tori shook her head. This couldn't be happening. Any minute she was going to wake up and find out that none of this was real. Back and forth, back and forth, she rocked the car until one of the tires finally caught on something and she was propelled forward. With a sigh, Tori settled into driving, sure that at any moment the tire she'd changed was going to fly down the road past her.

A little over an hour later, after tedious driving, and having her windshield assaulted by streams of slush from semitrailer trucks, she found the turnoff for Adam's home. It was a long private drive. She had to have traveled down it for five miles without seeing anything when suddenly an animal of some kind darted in front of her car. Tori slammed on her brakes, and even though she wasn't going that fast, her tires locked on the ice and sent the car into a ditch at the side of the road.

Tori sat there for a full thirty seconds before finally letting out one long primal scream of frustration. Getting out of the car, she slammed the door shut with all the force she could muster, then climbed out of the ditch and started down the road, muttering to herself the entire way. What was she doing here? Adam might not even *be* at the house. This might not even be the right road. There might not even be a house on this road.

But there was. She finally spotted it about three hundred yards in the distance. As she got closer, she saw a dim, flickering light coming from some of the windows. A dog started barking as Tori walked onto the porch and knocked on the door.

It opened and warm light poured on her from inside. Adam looked at her in surprise, and then a slow smile curved his mouth as his eyes moved down the length of her slush-and-grease spattered person.

"Don't you dare laugh at me," Tori warned him. "And if you're not glad to see me, keep it to yourself until after I've had a bath. I don't think I can take any more bad news right now."

He stood aside and let her in. Toby, whose tail was wagging madly, rubbed up against her. She started to pet him, but looked at her hand and decided against it. "Which way to a tub?"

"Off of the bedroom straight ahead."

"Thank you," she said with as much dignity as she could muster. "And I'd appreciate a shirt or something that I could wear."

"Where are your clothes?"

"God only knows." And with that she found the bathroom and ran a hot bath while she peeled the wet clothes from her body. As she sank into the hot water, a sigh escaped her lips. It had never felt this good before.

After soaking for a while, she let the water out of the tub and turned on the shower so she could wash her hair. As she was toweling it dry, there was a knock on the door. "I put a shirt out here on the bed for you."

"Thank you." Tori looked at herself in the mirror and felt her heart sink. What an entrance. If she could have left at that moment without having to face him, she would have. But she was stuck.

She found a dryer under the sink, plugged it in and blew her hair dry. Then she wrapped a towel around herself and went into the bedroom. The shirt was a long royal blue flannel one that came to just above her knees. She found a clean pair of white socks next to it and slipped them onto her feet. They hung past her toes by a good two inches, but they were warm, and covered her leg up to the knee. Still rolling the sleeves up, she walked out of the bedroom. Adam walked toward her and handed her a snifter of brandy. "You look like you could use this."

"Thank you."

Their fingers touched as she took it from him, and she felt the contact all the way up her arm. Her eyes roamed over his dear face. He looked tired. "This wasn't quite the entrance I'd imagined," she told him as she walked to the fire and stood in front of it.

"It was a little different," he agreed, sinking onto the couch, "even for you."

She stared into the fire for a moment, then looked back at him. "Do you want me to go?"

"I thought I wasn't supposed to tell you yet?"

"The bath helped. I can take it now."

His eyes rested on her for a long moment. "No, Tori, I don't want you to go."

She turned her face to the fire and closed her eyes in relief. Until that moment, she hadn't realized how much she'd dreaded his answer. "I . . ." she began.

"Tori."

She turned to find Adam next to her.

"Don't talk." He took her face in his hands and caressed her mouth with his. "Just don't talk," he said against her lips, pulling her body closer to his and finally lifting her into his arms and carrying her into the bedroom to lay her gently on the bed. As Tori watched, Adam lifted his sweater off over his head and then lowered himself next to her, pulling her into his arms, but not too close, as they lay facing one another. He reached up with a gentle hand and trailed his fingers down her smooth cheek, cherishing her with his eyes. "I love you," he said quietly. "I tried hard not to because I knew I could only bring you grief, but I go to bed at night with your image in my mind and I wake up with it in the morning. You're always with me." He moved his head closer to hers on the pillow and brushed his mouth against hers. "I want you with me. I want you to be my wife, in all of the ways it means to be husband and wife; I want to see our child growing inside you. I want to know that even if we're not together, you're bound to me in the same inextricable way I'm bound to you."

A tear trembled on her lashes. Adam touched it with his finger and looked into her eyes. "What's this?"

"I was so afraid you wouldn't want me. I don't think I've ever been so afraid of anything in my life."

"I've always wanted you," he said softly.

"Then why did you send me away?"

"Because I was trying to do what was best for you."

"Being away from you isn't best for me."

He pushed her hair away from her face. "I wish I understood what the hold is that you have over me. Ever since I saw you on that plane, I knew...." He shook his head.

Tori moved closer to him so that her body was pressed against his. "Make love to me," she whispered against the corner of his mouth.

Adam wrapped his arm around her. One hand went behind her head, his fingers tangling in her hair, as he pressed her mouth against his. The kiss grew deeper and deeper and more searching. Tori's fingers trailed down his strong back, pulling his body closer to hers, where it belonged.

Adam put his hand between them and gently unbuttoned the soft blue shirt. Still on their sides, he pushed the shirt off of one of her shoulders and caressed her skin with his mouth, his kisses gradually moving up the side of her throat to her ear where she could feel his breath, warm and sweet. He rolled her gently onto her back and raised himself over her, his eyes gazing tenderly into hers. "Are you all right?"

She reached out and cupped his face in her hands. "I love you, and as long as we're together, I'm all right."

"I can't believe you're really here," he said kissing her forehead. "You must have been reading my mind." His mouth captured hers again, as his hand slid down the length of her body, over her thigh and back up the smooth skin of the inside. As his fingers gently massaged her, his mouth lowered to her breast. Tori's fingers tangled in his hair, pulling his mouth even closer, aware of everything he was doing to her and feeling the passion building in her and spreading warmly through her body, then intensifying.

"Adam," she breathed.

He raised his body over hers, his mouth kissing hers, his tongue moving suggestively. Then he gently lowered himself on top of her, filling the void only he could create, and lay still for a moment as he looked into her eyes. Tori's fingers dug into his back and then slid over his hips as she pressed her body against his. Adam began moving inside her with exquisite slowness, and again she felt the passion build until she lost control of her own body from the force of the explosions that reverberated through her.

They both lay there in each other's arms, breathless and spent. Adam pushed her damp hair away from Tori's face and kissed her forehead, then held her closer against him. "It's a good thing we're already married."

Tori smiled. "It saved time."

Adam sighed, but didn't say anything.

"What's wrong?"

"We need to talk." He pulled a blanket up over them and then lay so that he was facing her on the pillow. "For the past year and a half, I've been selling off my grandfather's assets and making sure everything is as legitimate as possible. It's what he wanted, and I promised him I'd see it through."

Tori had guessed something like that was going on just from the information she'd been getting through the contacts she still had. "You mean you're not a genuine mobster? I wish you'd told me before...." She let her voice trail off.

Adam ruffled her hair, then grew more serious. "The problem is that it's going to take a few more months, and in the meantime I still have to deal with some very questionable characters."

"And?"

"And I want you out of it until I'm finished. I'd planned on coming for you when it was over with."

Tori raised up on her elbow. "I can't leave you now."

"It's only for a short time."

"No."

His eyes rested tenderly on hers. "I hope our children don't inherit your stubborn streak. I'm afraid that this time your stubbornness isn't going to work."

"Adam, don't make me leave you."

He rubbed his mouth against her forehead. "Oh, Tori, I do love you. And I know it's not going to be easy. But when we start our life together, I want to start clean. I don't want any of my grandfather's businesses hanging over our heads."

"What happens when they're legitimate? Will you still be running things?"

"No. Once everything is settled, my brother Joe, whom you haven't met yet, and Caroline are going to take over. I don't want any part of it. I'm an architect. That's all I've ever wanted to be."

"And then we can be together? Really together?"

"Really together."

She sighed. "How long is it going to take?"

"Six months. I have to do everything quietly. That's what takes the time."

"Six months," she repeated as she rolled onto her stomach and looked him in the eye. "I guess I can wait that long. I have a few matters of my own to clear up."

"Such as?"

"My job."

"Do you have to choose between it and me?"

"No. I've already chosen."

"I'm sorry."

She put her fingers lightly over his mouth. "It's all right, really. I knew in my heart this was going to happen eighteen months ago. I'm ready for it."

As she lay her head on his chest, Adam thoughtfully rubbed his chin against her hair. This was going to be the hardest six months he'd ever had.

Six and a half months later, Tori was walking down the street, deep in thought. She hadn't once seen or heard from Adam in all that time, and though she'd been tempted to call him just to hear his voice, she hadn't because that was the way he wanted it.

There were days when she was positive he was going to come for her, and then there were days when she was sure he wasn't. She thought about how she'd shown up on his doorstep and literally forced her way into his life that night in Connecticut, cringing at her own behavior one minute, and being sure she'd done the right thing the next.

One sunny summer afternoon, as she was walking down the street oblivious to her surroundings, a car suddenly pulled in front of her. She stopped walking and just stood there as Adam got out of the car and stood next to it. Tori swallowed hard at the sight of him, so tall and strong, and looking at her with an expression that told her more than words how much he loved her.

Adam walked over to Tori and folded her in his arms. "It's over," he said quietly against her hair. "Let's go home."

*   *   *   *   *

A breathtaking roller coaster of adventure, passion and danger in the dazzling Roaring Twenties!

SCANDALOUS SPIRITS

ERIN YORKE

Running from unspeakable danger, she found shelter—and desire—in the arms of a reckless stranger.

FOUR UNIQUE SERIES
FOR EVERY WOMAN YOU ARE...

Silhouette Romance

Love, at its most tender, provocative, emotional... in stories that will make you laugh and cry while bringing you the magic of falling in love.

6 titles per month

Silhouette Special Edition

Sophisticated, substantial and packed with emotion, these powerful novels of life and love will capture your imagination and steal your heart.

6 titles per month

Silhouette Desire

Open the door to romance and passion. Humorous, emotional, compelling—yet always a believable and sensuous story—Silhouette Desire never fails to deliver on the promise of love.

6 titles per month

Silhouette Intimate Moments

Enter a world of excitement, of romance heightened by suspense, adventure and the passions every woman dreams of. Let us sweep you away.

4 titles per month

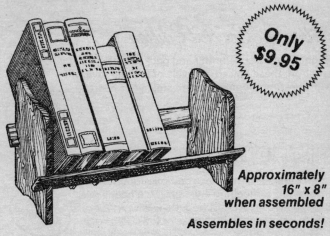

COMING NEXT MONTH

#556 NEVER LOVE A COWBOY—Rita Rainville
Anne Sheldon thought she was resigned to widowhood and could live off
her happy memories, but Ben Benedict knew better. He was sure Anne
deserved a future as well as a past—a future that included him.

#557 DONOVAN'S MERMAID—Helen R. Myers
Chief of police Sam Donovan was Gulls Drift's most confirmed bachelor
until he rescued Miranda Paley from the Gulf of Mexico. Now Sam's heart
needed rescuing from Randi's captivating smile. Would the little town of
Gulls Drift ever be the same?

#558 A KISS IS STILL A KISS—Colleen Christie
Kurt Lawrence needed feisty Margo Shepherd to help him revamp his
video chain. But after an impulsive kiss and a case of mistaken identity,
how could he assure her he was strictly business? Especially when the
memory of her lips had him longing to mix business with pleasure....

#559 UNDER A DESERT SKY—Arlene James
Jamie Goff had been born in the Nevada desert, and her heart had always
belonged under an endless sky. But when citified Bronson Taylor laid
claim to her love, Jamie was torn—Bron must return to the city. Would
Jamie have to choose between her two loves?

#560 THE OUTSIDER—Stella Bagwell
Luke Chandler had arrived just in the nick of time to save
Faith Galloway's ranch, but Faith felt more than gratitude for her
mysterious new employee. Was Faith's love strong enough to convince the
handsome drifter that it was time to settle down?

#561 WIFE WANTED—Terri Herrington
Tycoon Joe Dillon had launched the perfect advertising campaign to find
himself a wife, but the woman he wanted hadn't applied for the job. He'd
have to do some powerful persuading to show "happily single"
Brit Alexander that the man behind the slogans had a heart of gold....

Silhouette Romance™

Legendary Lovers Trilogy

BY DEBBIE MACOMBER....

ONCE UPON A TIME, in a land not so far away, there lived a girl, Debbie Macomber, who grew up dreaming of castles, white knights and princes on fiery steeds. Her family was an ordinary one with a mother and father and one wicked brother, who sold copies of her diary to all the boys in her junior high class.

One day, when Debbie was only nineteen, a handsome electrician drove by in a shiny black convertible. Now Debbie knew a prince when she saw one, and before long they lived in a two-bedroom cottage surrounded by a white picket fence.

As often happens when a damsel fair meets her prince charming, children followed, and soon the two-bedroom cottage became a four-bedroom castle. The kingdom flourished and prospered, and between soccer games and car pools, ballet classes and clarinet lessons, Debbie thought about love and enchantment and the magic of romance.

One day Debbie said, "What this country needs is a good fairy tale." She remembered how well her diary had sold and she dreamed again of castles, white knights and princes on fiery steeds. And so the stories of Cinderella, Beauty and the Beast, and Snow White were reborn....

Look for Debbie Macomber's *Legendary Lovers* trilogy from Silhouette Romance: *Cindy and the Prince* (January, 1988); *Some Kind of Wonderful* (March, 1988); *Almost Paradise* (May, 1988). Don't miss them!